PHANTOMS ON THE BOOKSHELVES

JACQUES BONNET

PHANTOMS
ON THE BOOKSHELVES

Translated from the French by
Siân Reynolds

Introduction by James Salter

THE OVERLOOK PRESS
NEW YORK, NY

This edition first published in hardcover in the United States in 2012 by

The Overlook Press, Peter Mayer Publishers, Inc.
141 Wooster Street
New York, NY 10012
www.overlookpress.com
For bulk and special sales contact sales@overlookny.com

First published in the French language as *Des bibliothèques pleines de fantômes*
by Éditions Denoël, Paris
Copyright © Éditions Denoël, 2008
English translation copyright © 2010 by Siân Reynolds

This book is supported by the French Ministry of Foreign Affairs,
as part of the Burgess programme run by the Cultural Department of
the French Embassy in London

Liberté • Égalité • Fraternité
RÉPUBLIQUE FRANÇAISE

Cataloging-in-Publication data is available from the Library of Congress

Manufactured in the United States of America
ISBN 978-1-59020-759-8

1 3 5 7 9 10 8 6 4 2

To Luiz Dantas

CONTENTS

TRANSLATOR'S AND EDITOR'S NOTE

This is a book about books. It contains many titles in several languages. In the original, Jacques Bonnet lists details of the edition sitting on his bookshelves, which is usually in French: date, publisher, translator. The policy adopted for the translation is that, except for very well-known titles, such as *War and Peace*, the titles of books originally written in French (or other languages) are kept in the text, followed immediately either by the title, in italics, of the English translation, if there is one; or by a literal translation of the title, in roman type, if none exists. There is a full bibliography with dates and details at the end for readers who would like to follow up any titles: where possible the English edition is cited.

After owning books, almost the next best thing
is talking about them.

CHARLES NODIER

INTRODUCTION

As Anthony Burgess once commented, there is no better reason for not reading a book than having it, but an exception should be made for this one, which appears at a time when books and literature as we have known them are undergoing a great and perhaps catastrophic change. A tide is coming in and the kingdom of books, with their white pages and endpapers, their promise of solitude and discovery, is in danger, after an existence of five hundred years, of being washed away. The physical possession of a book may become of little significance. Access to it will be what matters and when the book is closed, so to speak, it will disappear into the cyber. It will be like the genie – summonable but unreal. The private library of Jacques Bonnet, however, comprised of more than forty thousand volumes, is utterly real. Assembled according to his own interests, idiosyncratic, it came into being more or less incidentally over some four decades, through a love of reading and a disinclination to part with a book after it was acquired. Among other things, he might need it some day.

Under the pretence of writing about this library, its origins, contents and organization, he has written instead this often witty tribute to and perhaps requiem for a life built around reading that summons up all the magical and seductive power of books. You recognize, with a kind of terrible joy, all that you haven't read and that you would like to read. Titles and names strike what can only be called chords of desire. In these pages, as at a fabulous party, you are introduced to writers who have not been translated into English, or barely. Hugues Rebell, Milan Fust, Anders Nygren, Kafū Nagai (1879–1959), the Japanese writer of the floating world about whom Edward Seidensticker wrote *Kafu the Scribbler*, or Osamu Dazai, "tubercular and desperate", who attempted suicide three or four times, the last time successfully with his mistress. To these as well as to writers more famous, and to incredible characters: Count Serlon de Savigny and his beautiful fencing-champion mistress, Hauteclaire Stassin, who together murder the count's wife and live happily ever after in Jules Barbey d'Aurevilly's *Happiness in Crime*, or Edvarda, the trader's daughter in Knut Hamsun's *Pan*, who sometimes came to the cabin where Lieutenant Thomas Glahn lived near the forest with his dog, Aesop.

Bonnet did not resist these books. They became, in a way, part of him, and he manages to bring up the question of what one has read, what one should read, what one remembers and, in a para-doxical way, what is the use of it. This last question can be dealt with more easily: Reading has the power not only to demolish time and span the ages, but also the capacity to make one feel more human – human meaning at one with humanity – and possibly less savage. Bonnet admits that he has not read all his books which, even at the rate of two or three a week, would take the better part of a century. Some he has read and forgotten, others he remembers, although not always perfectly – indelible, however, are "the two wild duck feathers which the lieutenant, Thomas Glahn, *with the blazing eyes of a wild beast* would receive two years later folded into a sheet of paper embossed with a coat of arms" – and a great number of books he has only glanced at or not read at all. As he describes it himself, books that he has acquired, that is, has bought rather than received because of his occupation as a writer and editor, can end up in one of three ways:

> They may be read immediately, or pretty soon; they may be put off for reading later (and that could mean weeks, months and even years, if circumstances are particularly unfavourable, or the number of incoming books is too great – what I call my "to read" pile). Or they may go straight on to the shelf.

He goes on to say that even these books immediately shelved have, in a sense, been "read". He knows what they are and where they are; they can be of use one day. He is able, of course, to read quickly since this has long been his work, but some books should not be read quickly. One often hears the expression "I couldn't put it down", but there are books that you have to put down. Books should be read at the speed they deserve, he properly notes. There are books that can be skimmed and fully grasped and others that only yield themselves, so to speak, on the second or even third reading.

All of this is normal, and you have probably formed an image of a pallid bookworm, serious and solitary. Bonnet is not like this. He is, to the contrary, convivial, good-natured, even jaunty. He has spent his life as an editor, as a journalist for *Le Monde* and *L'Express*, and as an art historian writing a book on the life and paintings of Lorenzo Lotto. These are what might be called the visible occupations. At the same time, and much of the time, he has read. He has always read. He likes to read, as he says, "anywhere and in any position" although for him – and he is a voluptuary in this regard – the ideal is lying down or, as he elsewhere mentions, in the bath. I have never seen him reading although I remember that the one visit I made to his Paris apartment was like walking into La Hune; the walls were completely covered with bookshelves and the shelves were filled with books. This was fifteen or twenty years ago, and I don't know if there was then the full complement of books, nor do I know what forty thousand books would look like, but it was an apartment dedicated to them. I didn't wonder at the time how they were arranged, and I did not consider what, after the joy of acquisition, must be an overwhelming reality for the owner of a large library; that it is almost impossible to move, both from the point of view of finding another place large enough as well as actually moving all the books, packing, transporting and reshelving them.

A private library of good size is an insolent form of riches, and the desire to have more books is difficult to rationalize, especially in view of the fact that you do not or cannot read them all but, as

Bonnet makes clear, still you might. The bibliophile is, after all, like a sultan or khan who has countless wives already but another two or three are always irresistible. Reading is a pastime and can be regarded as such, but it can also be supremely important. Walter Benjamin expressed it off-handedly; he read, he said, "just to get in touch". I take this to mean in touch with things otherwise impossible to embrace rather than merely stay abreast of, although a certain ambiguity is the mark of accomplished writers. Benjamin's life ended tragically. He fled from the Nazis but was trapped, unable to cross into Spain, and he committed suicide, but that was the end only of his mortal life. He exists still with a kind of shy radiance and the continued interest and esteem of readers. He is dead like everyone else, except that he is not. You might say the same of a movie star except that it seems to me that stars are viewed years after with a kindly curiosity. They are antique and perhaps still charming. A writer does not age in the same way. He or she is not imprisoned in a performance.

Books, as Bonnet comments, are expensive to buy and worth very little if you try to sell them. The fate of a private library after the death of its owner is almost always to be scattered. There are exceptions, like the library assembled in Hamburg by Aby Warburg that was moved to London in 1933 to keep it out of the hands of the Nazis, and that became the heart of an institute for Renaissance studies. But even great libraries, those of schools and cities, have come to ruin, destroyed by fire, war, or decree: Alexandria's famous library, Dresden's in 1945, others. An emperor of China, Qin Shi Huangdi, you will learn, the builder of the Great Wall, also ordered the destruction of all books that did not concern themselves with medicine, agriculture or divination. There were a number of sages who preferred to die rather than destroy their libraries.

The love of books, the possession of them, can be thought of as an extension of one's self or being, not separate from a love of life but rather as an extra dimension of it, and even of what comes after. "Paradise is a library", as Borges said.

The writers of books are companions in one's life and as such are often more interesting than other companions. Men on their way to execution are sometimes consoled by passages from the Bible, which is really a book written by great, if unknown writers. There are many writers and many of some magnitude, like the stars in the heavens, some visible and some not, but they shed glory, as Bonnet makes clear without the least attempt at persuasion.

James Salter

On 1 September 1932, the Portuguese newspaper O *Século* carried an advertisement for the post of librarian-curator at the Condes de Castro Guimarães Museum, in Cascais, a little town on the coast about thirty kilometres from Lisbon. On 16 September, the poet Fernando Pessoa sent the local authority a letter applying for the post. The six-page document was later reproduced in a book by Maria José de Lancastre, *Fernando Pessoa, uma fotobiografia* (*Fernando Pessoa: photographic documentation*), published in 1981 by Imprensa Nacional-Casa da Moeda and the Centro de Estudios Pessoanos, which I bought for 500 *escudos* in a bookshop in Coimbra in November 1983. It was the only copy they had. In the town's cafés in those days there was still a ledge under the table where you could put your hat, and I remember seeing a woman go past in the street with a sewing machine balanced on her head. The Portuguese text of the letter is reproduced in *Fernando Pessoa* in characters far too tiny for anyone without good Portuguese to decipher.

Pessoa, who was tired of translating commercial correspondence for import-export firms in Lisbon, on a wage that scarcely allowed him to survive and get (moderately) drunk every day, felt the urge to change his way of life and leave his flat at 16, Coelho da Rocha Street for a small town near Lisbon. In my copy

7

of the book, a few pages before the letter, there is a photograph of Pessoa drinking a glass of red wine in the shop owned by the wine merchant Abel Ferreira da Fonseca. Behind him you can see casks of Clairette, Abafado, Moscatel, Ginginha and so on. This was the snapshot which Pessoa sent in September 1929 to Ophelia Queiroz, the only romantic relationship he is known to have had. The dedication reads: "Fernando Pessoa, em flagrante delitro", or "Fernando Pessoa in flagrante with a litre". Sending the photograph had marked the renewal of a connection broken off nine years earlier, and which would end, permanently this time, six months later. At least, it ended materially. Ophelia never married, and she recounted that shortly before his death, Pessoa, on meeting his nephew Carlos, had asked him, "How is Ophelia?", then, his eyes filled with tears, had grasped his hands and added: "Oh what a fine soul, a fine soul!"

There are two other editions of Maria José de Lancastre's album on my bookshelves. An Italian version (Adelphi, 1988) has been abridged – 164 pages instead of 322! – and the letter appears only in a reduced form, just the first and last pages, making it even less legible than in the original book. On the other hand, it does show a photo of the museum in question, the neo-Gothic villa of Count Castro Guimarães. By contrast, the French version (translated by Pierre Léglise-Costa, published by Christian Bourgois in 1990) reproduces in their entirety the documents published in the original edition, and adds a translation of the letter of application. This document, which really ought to be quoted in full, is a heartrending example of the frequent gaps that exist between the two worlds of the artist, the one in which he lives mentally – at the risk perhaps of losing himself – and the world he inhabits every day. Let us content ourselves here with the final paragraph:

The documents cited in paragraph 1 above, and enclosed herewith, are more than adequate evidence to convey the applicant's knowledge of English. As for his knowledge of French, the applicant is of the view that in the absence of truly valid documents (such as those he can produce for English) the best thing he can do is to attach an extract from the magazine *Contemporanea* no. 7, where on pp. 20 and 21 are published three songs which he wrote in French – "*Trois chansons mortes*" (Three dead songs). In the further particulars for the post, it states that the librarian-curator should be a person of "recognized competence and appropriateness". The degree of competence and appropriateness implicit in the qualifications indicated as preferable in the paragraphs of the article will therefore be supported by documentary proof in the documents concerning each paragraph, [but] competence and appropriateness are not provable by document. They even include elements such as physical appearance and education, which are of themselves non-documentable.

Cascais 16 September 1932

Fernando Nogueira Pessoa

The appointing committee, chaired by the mayor of Cascais, and no doubt baffled by this unaccustomed rhetoric, was not convinced; it prudently chose another candidate, whom Pessoa's biographers usually describe rather vaguely as "an obscure painter".

1

TENS OF THOUSANDS OF BOOKS

Some people are fond of horses, others of wild animals; in my
case, I have been possessed since childhood by a prodigious
desire to buy and own books.

JULIAN THE APOSTATE

About fifteen years ago, the Paris publishing house I was working for published a novel by the great Italian writer and critic
Giuseppe Pontiggia. Probably nobody else who could stammer
out a few words of Italian was available that particular evening, so
I was asked to "look after" him. We met for dinner in a restaurant
(Russian as it happened) near the Vavin crossroads. We got on
well, particularly since he and his wife Lucia spoke French much
better than I did Italian. After the first few minutes of conversation, we realized we had something in common, which transformed the interest of the evening: we both owned a monstrous
personal library of several tens of thousands of books – not one of
those bibliophile libraries containing works so valuable that their
owner never opens them for fear of damaging them, no, I'm talking about a working library, the kind where you don't hesitate to
write on your books, or read them in the bath; a library that results

from keeping everything you have ever read – including paper-backs and perhaps several editions of the same title – as well as the ones you mean to read one day. A non-specialist library, or rather one specialized in so many areas that it becomes a general one. We spent the entire meal discussing both the enjoyment and the curse of our lot. Books are expensive to buy, but worth nothing if you try to sell them second-hand; they become impossibly dear once they are out of print; they are heavy to carry, gather dust, are vulnerable to damp and mice, and once you have acquired a certain number they make it impossible to move house; they need a workable retrieval system if you want to use them, and above all they take up room.

I once had a bathroom full of bookshelves, which made it impossible to take a shower, and meant running a bath with the window open because of the condensation; and I also kept them in my kitchen, which made it out of the question to use certain strong-smelling foodstuffs. As was the case for many of my colleagues, it was years before I could afford a living space equal to my book-collecting ambitions. Only the wall above my bed has always been spared from bookshelves, as the consequence of an ancient trauma. I learnt, long ago, the circumstances of the death of the composer Charles-Valentin Alkan, sometimes described as the "Berlioz of the piano", who was found on 30 March, 1888 crushed to death by his own bookshelves. Every craft guild used to have its patron saint and martyr, so Alkan the elder, the virtuoso pianist whom Liszt admired, and who inherited Chopin's pupils from him, must surely be the patron saint of demented book collectors. As in the Greek myths, there are several variants of his tragic end, and a different one suggests he was the victim of a heavy umbrella-stand, but since there is room for doubt, I prefer my version. I also possess in my record collection, in homage to this tutelary martyr to our gentle and inoffensive obsession, a classic R.C.A. vinyl of his Grande Sonate, "The Four Ages", recorded in January 1979 by Pierre Reach.

That evening in Paris, Pontiggia and I had come face to face with another member of our clandestine confraternity, of necessity a limited one, given the conditions one has to fulfil, and we were able to tackle a number of serious questions of which ordinary mortals remain in complete ignorance. Why, for instance, does it so often happen that the out-of-print book you ordered the moment you received the bookseller's catalogue turns out – already – to be unavailable after all? Or, how should you classify your books? By alphabetical order, by genre, by language, chronologically, or – why not? – according to an invisible web of affinities of the Warburg kind (more of this in Chapter 3), mysterious to everyone except the owner? Gilbert Lely, the poet and specialist on Sade, apparently always kept one hundred books on his shelves, not a single one more, and whenever he bought one book he jettisoned another. Georges Perec tells the story of one of his friends who decided, for some reason as surreal as it is incomprehensible, on the ideal number as 361, but could never decide how to count books that came in several volumes, or compendia like the Pléiade editions, which contain several books in one.

We spent some happy moments, Pontiggia and I, comparing the reactions of occasional visitors to a sight they found astonishing. After the "oohs and ahs" there inevitably came the same questions: "How many have you got?" "Have you read them all?" "How do you find your way around them?" – and so on. For us, by contrast, it would be more of a surprise to go into someone's house and find no books at all, or find no more than a skeleton library belonging to a so-called colleague; or, alternatively, a beautifully arranged set of volumes, protected by glass-fronted bookcases, which you sense at once are entirely for show.

By the end of the evening, with the help of the vodka, we had dreamed up an association of owners of private libraries containing over twenty thousand books – exactly the number of Professor Ermanno Finzi-Contini's books in Giorgio Bassani's novel, *The Garden of the Finzi-Continis*. The association would have the function of defending the interests of this little-known minority. Our association never saw the light of day, but from that evening on, we maintained a friendly complicity, which ended only with the premature death of my friend Giuseppe "Peppo" Pontiggia in June 2003.

But how does one get to be the owner of so many books? Individual answers would probably be of many kinds: family tradition ("May I be allowed to repeat that my father's library was the capital event in my life. The truth is that I have never left it" – Borges); prize-winning schooldays; a budding academic career;

or a mixture of all those elements. In my case, none of these apply. Instead it was a heartfelt desire to fulfil Borges's definition of a book collection, "Paradise is a library", or Bachelard's, "Doesn't paradise consist of a huge library?" – although I prefer, with agnostic prudence, to turn these definitions inside out: the library is what brings us closest to paradise on earth.

Before that, came the discovery of reading – which penetrated, like a shaft of sunlight, through the gloomy atmosphere of a provincial childhood of the 1960s. One day, someone will write a book about the boredom of those years, when our fathers were rebuilding the French economy (and helping themselves, on the way) while their wives and children were still living in the nineteenth century. The so-called "thirty glorious years" (1945–75) weren't glorious for everyone. Yes, French women had the vote at last, but their legal status was still very largely defined by marriage; married women couldn't own a chequebook, for example. In the provincial petite bourgeoisie where I was brought up, women still looked after home and children, and depended on the head of the family for their housekeeping money. As for the children, they were, to put it briefly, daily confronted with the authority principle. To take just one example: in 1967 it was still forbidden to bring a daily newspaper – even serious ones like *Le Figaro*, *Combat* or *Le Monde* – into a French state *lycée*. Family discussions were rare, and one's parents' decisions were not over-burdened by rational considerations. The tedium of childhood could be fought only by two things: sport or reading. And reading was something like the river flowing through the Garden of Eden, its four watercourses heading off toward the four horizons. Reading scorns distance, and could transport me instantly into the most faraway countries with the strangest customs. And it did the same for centuries of the past: I had only to open a book to be able to walk through seventeenth-century Paris, at the risk of having a chamber-pot emptied over my head, to defend the walls of Byzantium as they tottered before falling to the Ottomans, or to stroll through Pompeii the night before it was buried under a tidal wave of ash and lava. I noticed after a while that books were not only a salutary method of escape, they also contained tools that made it possible to decode the reality around me. The ambitious petit-bourgeois milieu of my youth wanted to consolidate its upward mobility, and in order to do so was prepared to support its children throughout their education. It was time to move out of trade and into the law, medicine, or finance. These were the real roots of May '68: the younger generation had become more intelligent, or at any rate better educated than its parents (not difficult) and was starting to ask unprecedented questions which, although by no means absurd, did not receive even the beginnings of an answer until the first cobblestones began to fly. Escape and knowledge: it all came from books. I have retained from that time an eternal gratitude, a sort of moral debt towards them, one I have still not finished paying. It was also a way of sliding off the family rails. Hence my ambition – as good as any other, after all – to turn my life to advantage by reading all the books in the world.

But why keep tens of thousands of books in one's private library? Why could paradise not consist simply of a few shelves? For some people, a single book is enough! For others, the libraries that already exist would suffice. But as Robert Musil explained, that doesn't suit everyone. ("I can't work in public libraries, because smoking is forbidden. That makes sense, doesn't it? But when I read at home, I don't smoke." – *Diaries*)

Then there was the sequence of chance moves which led me to take various jobs in the book trade. Hence my taste for complete sets (by author, subject, collection, period, country, and so on) and an extreme difficulty in parting with a book once read (who knows whether, in the future, I might need a book I found boring first time round?). At any rate, the choice between what to keep and what to throw out takes a kind of energy I have always been unwilling to expend (barring a few exceptions, admittedly). Finally, there was the urge to have ready to hand all the books, paintings, music and films I possibly could, as elements of internal freedom. This was of course long before the internet made it all readily available. It is infinitely easier now than in the past to find an out-of-print volume via the AbeBooks website, which puts you in touch with the catalogues of 13,500 second-hand bookshops from all over the world – but you will only find there what you are already looking for: it's not the same at all as thumbing through a bookseller's booth on the banks of the Seine and turning up a book you have never heard of before.

Like Shalamov, the author of *Kolyma Tales* ("I can't remember learning to read and I am bold enough to think I must always have been able to"), I have no memory of the moment I learnt to read, unlike some people, who can recall what it was like "before", such as a Brazilian friend, who claims to remember – unless he has been told this by his family – a time when he pretended to read aloud texts he could not possibly have understood. At any rate, starting from this long-forgotten moment, I read avidly everything that passed in front of my eyes, using any free time left over from playing football. From this vague magma of random readings, only a few memories now swim up: the adventures of Bob Morane (forerunner of the rather more spicy secret agent O.S.S. 117, whom I encountered in adolescence); or romantic novels by Delly (about girls who were poor and beautiful and fell in love with young men who inevitably turned out to be the sons of princes kidnapped in childhood – or else about young men, who were poor and handsome and fell for girls who turned out to be ... you get the picture). Then there was Captain Corcoran and Louison, his tame tiger, the gentleman robber Arsène Lupin, always immaculately turned out – I can still see the disturbing cover of *L'Ile aux trente cercueils* (*Coffin Island*), a book issued in instalments and found in our attic – or Louis Garneray, a painter of marine life and chronicler of Surcouf the corsair and his shipmates. I systematically refused – for reasons that remain a mystery to me today – to read any of my set books at school, which meant I had to wait an extra ten years before discovering Montaigne, Racine, Diderot or Balzac.

Among the few exceptions to survive from this period are the *Adventures of Robinson Crusoe,* whose fate of organized solitude already fascinated me, and the books of the only authors in my grandfather's small library, whom he read and reread all his life: Alexandre Dumas and Charles Dickens. I also read voraciously the three magazines to which my grandparents subscribed: *Le Chasseur français* (The French hunter): stories about guns and dogs did not greatly appeal to me, but there was a section called "Jokes and epigrams" which I loved; *Historia,* where I found plenty of encouragement to dream about the enigma of the man in the iron mask, or the destiny of the lost dauphin, Louis XVII, to mourn the tragic lot of Marie-Antoinette or the duc d'Enghien, or to wonder at the strange fate of Fouquet, ending his life in the Pinerolo fortress, after the splendour of Vaux-le-Vicomte; and lastly, *Reader's Digest,* in which I discovered the great events of the century, the horrors of the Great War, and what were then called concentration camps, telling myself there would never be any more anti-Semitism or genocide in the world – on which count I was of course wrong.

So you see, I devoured quite indiscriminately anything that was printed, and not very much of it stuck, except a habit of reading which had somehow to be channelled. It was only when, like many French teenagers of my generation, I read Boris Vian's *L'Ecume des jours (Froth on the Daydream)* at the age of about fifteen that I discovered that novels could be more than an adventure story to dream about, and that the word "literature" started to mean something. Vian did have the signal advantage of being a writer whose name was spread by word of mouth; he was never on the school syllabus.

2

BIBLIOMANIA

Of what interest to me are those countless books and
libraries, whose owners have scarcely read the
labels in their whole lifetime?

SENECA

There are plenty of libraries to be found in novels. Sometimes they
are even a central element – the library of the Benedictine abbey
in *The Name of the Rose*, Des Esseintes's library in *A Rebours* (*Against
Nature*), by J. K. Huysmans, or the one belonging to the Sinologist
Peter Kien in Elias Canetti's *Auto-da-fé*, not to mention the "definitive" 12,000 volumes owned by Captain Nemo in Jules Verne's
Twenty Thousand Leagues under the Sea. But I know of only one novel
in which virtually every character is a bibliomaniac: Carlos Maria
Dominguez's *La Casa de papel* (*The Paper House*). The narrator is
himself haunted by the proliferation of his books ("They are
advancing silently, innocently, through my house. There is no way
I can stop them"), and finally succeeds in his quest to find another
bibliomaniac, Carlos Bauer, only to discover that the latter has
already given up the struggle: "Classifying twenty thousand
volumes is no easy matter […] You have to have a strict respect for

order, an almost superhuman respect, I would say". Bauer's fragile mental equilibrium cannot survive the loss of the card index without which his library has become impenetrable. So he uses his books to build a house (*la casa de papel*) on a beach far away from everything, and then destroys it, trying to find a book by Joseph Conrad (*The Shadow Line*), which someone has asked him to return.

But how does anyone manage to acquire so many thousands of books, which end up posing as many problems for their owner? There are various explanations, none of them exclusive – depending on the kind of bibliomaniac we are talking about. The term "bibliomaniac" can be applied to a wide range of personalities. They can be divided into two principal categories: collectors and manic readers.

Collectors can further be sub-divided into specialists and the all-purpose variety. The former will devote themselves to one author: in 1924, Tristan Bernard put up for sale the 173 editions of *Paul et Virginie* (*Paul and Virginia*) by Bernardin de Saint-Pierre which he had patiently collected; or perhaps a period or genre (Pierre-Jean Rémy collected eighteenth-century libertine novels); or a topic, a particular kind of binding, and so on. Christian Galantaris in his *Manuel de bibliophilie* (Handbook of bibliophilia) quotes two examples: Henry C. Folger (1857–1930), an associate of John D. Rockefeller, who bought up all the past editions of Shakespeare he could find (owning as many as eighteen copies of the same edition), and putting together a collection as large as that in the library of the British Museum (now the British Library). The second was James Douglas (1657–1742), an English doctor whose admiration for the works of Horace led him to possess 450 editions of his works, from the Milan edition of 1493 to one produced in 1739, the date of publication of his *Catalogue*. And there are even more eccentric cases, such as the collector who amassed only books by writers starting with B, or whose first name was Jules, like his own.

The rarity value of a book can also be a factor in its choice. So in his *Mélanges tirés d'une petite bibliothèque* (Gleanings from a small library), published in Paris by Crapelet in 1829, one senses the pride Charles Nodier felt in owning one of only seven or eight copies of the *Oeuvres diverses d'un auteur de sept ans* (Various works by a seven-year-old author), published "without any indication of place and date", but probably in Paris, by the Imprimerie Royale in 1678. Nodier explains, "This book, which contains a few schoolbook exercises and letters written by the little duc de Maine, was printed by his governess, Mme de Maintenon, and his tutor, M. de Ragois".

Even I, although I do not count myself a real bibliophile, am quite moved to think I own copy number 696 of the four-volume catalogue of the works of Edgar Degas edited by P. A. Lemoine, *Degas et son oeuvre* (Degas and his works), published by Paul Brame/ C. M. de Hauke, Arts et Métiers graphiques, in Paris in 1946–9. This was not quite as exclusively produced as Charles Nodier's rarity, being in an edition of 950 copies (plus fifty "not for sale") printed on watermarked Arches paper. But it was really the interest of Degas's works that was the decisive factor, outweighing even the price. And I do have one precious and mysterious possession, whose riddle I hope to solve one day. This is a copy of a book called *Sagesse et chimères* (Wisdom and fantasies) by René Bertrand, with a preface by Jean Cocteau. The book was published by Grasset in 1953, but with a white Gallimard cover which has nothing to do with it, since it carries the title *Kleist ou la fascination de la mort* (Kleist or fascination with death) by one Jean-Martin Pradès. One might imagine that there was some mix-up at the printers between two books published respectively by Gallimard and Grasset, and that somehow the wrong cover had been attached – which would be mystery enough. But there are two details which complicate matters even further: the endpaper inside the book indicates one printer: "This edition (1st impression) was completed on 2 November 1953 for Bernard Grasset, Publishers, Paris, by Floch Printers, Mayenne, etc", while the cover carries a note that it was printed at another, by "Didot et Cie, Paris XIe, Roq-08-60". What is more, there is no mention of a work on Kleist by Jean-Martin Pradès in the Gallimard catalogue, nor indeed anywhere else, not in any bibliography of Kleist, not even in the catalogue of the French National Library, the Bibliothèque Nationale de France. Nor can I find any trace anywhere of the said Jean-Martin Pradès. How did this Grasset title come to have a Gallimard cover for a non-existent book by an entirely unknown author? Where could this odd volume have come from?

There is a lithograph by Daumier called "The book-lover in heaven" (from *Le Charivari*, 5 November, 1844) which perfectly illustrates the fascination rarity holds for the bibliophile. It shows a man thumbing through a little book and explaining to another book-lover, "I can't tell you how happy I am … I've just found the 1780 Amsterdam edition of Horace for fifty *écus* – it's very valuable, because every page is covered with misprints!"

The mania for collecting can easily turn simply into accumulating. All one has to do is develop one collecting interest after another, and so on. But collectors of a particular category of articles almost always lose interest once they have reached their goal. When the collection is complete, what else is there to do? With nothing else to look for, the fascination of the thing completely evaporates. The collector contemplates the collection for a while (and through the collection, the image of him or herself, persevering and eventually reaching the desired goal) then neglects it, puts it aside, or gets rid of it, and starts another. The important thing is the chase. One can't help thinking of the beaming face of Mr Gutman (Sydney Greenstreet) at the end of the film *The Maltese Falcon*, when he realizes that the object on which he has finally laid his hands is a fake ("It's a phoney!") and that he is going to have to return to Istanbul in search of the original. ("Well, sir, what do you suggest, we stand here and shed tears and call each other names, or shall we go to Istanbul?") The chase is on again. If the falcon found by Sam Spade (Humphrey Bogart) had been authentic – the solid golden bird which the Knights of Malta presented to Charles V in 1539 – the fat man's life would have lost all meaning and he would have had to look for something else. Failure makes it possible to avoid the effort: he simply carries on as before.

People who merely accumulate books give the impression that they have lost sight of any numerical limits and have completely abandoned any idea of reading those they have. Galantaris quotes the case of Sir Richard Heber (1774–1833), who owned 300,000 books divided between five different libraries in England and on the continent, each of which had spread itself over five different lodgings: "The books were omnipresent, forming veritable forests, with paths, avenues, groves and tracks, in which one kept bumping into piles and columns of books spilling out from the shelves and heaped up on tables, chairs and the floor". As for Antoine-Marie-Henri Boulard (1754–1825), a former notary and mayor of the VIIIth arrondissement of Paris under Napoleon, he had started out by trying to save the books which confiscations and revolutionary appropriations had released on to the market, and ended up filling the nine or ten buildings which he had to acquire in order to house his 600,000 volumes. When his sons arranged for the sale of these books between 1828 and 1832, it apparently resulted in the flooding of the second-hand market in bookshops and *bouquinistes'* booths, so that prices collapsed, and remained low for several years. A certain French haut-couturier of German origin (he wears dark glasses, has a pony tail, and is aged 75, though he does not like to have that mentioned) owns up to having 300,000 books, divided among his five houses.

The other major kind of bibliomania is that of the compulsive reader. Not that people in the first category don't read, but their chief interest lies elsewhere. And not that people in the second category don't accumulate books, but this is a consequence of their mania rather than their original intention. In their case, it starts with the itch to read and a wide-ranging curiosity, which does not necessarily imply book collecting, since they could always consult works in libraries, or borrow them, or sell them again after buying them. But the reading bibliomaniac wants to hold on to the physical object, to keep it ready to hand. Carlos Maria Dominguez's narrator gives a good idea of this phenomenon, of the reader who is attached not only to reading but to the object that allowed him to do it:

> I have often asked myself why I keep books that could only ever be of any use in a distant future, titles remote from my usual concerns, those I have read once and will not open again for many years, if ever! But how could I throw away *The Call of the Wild*, for example, without destroying one of the building bricks of my childhood, or *Zorba the Greek*, which brought my adolescence to a tear-stained end, *The Twenty-Fifth Hour* [by Virgil Gheorghiu] and all those other volumes consigned long since to the topmost shelves, where they lie untouched and silent, preserved by the sacred fidelity we have sworn to them.

Alberto Manguel says much the same thing:

As I build pile after pile of familiar volumes [...] I wonder, as I have wondered every other time, why I keep so many books that I know I will not read again? I tell myself that, every time I get rid of a book, I find a few days later that this is precisely the book I'm looking for. I tell myself that there are no books (or very, very few) in which I have found nothing at all to interest me (*A History of Reading*).

Manguel is at one on this with Pliny the Elder: "It is very rarely that a bad book does not contain some merit for the cultivated man". In these two reasons not to part with a book – the recall of a long-lost sentiment, or some possible interest in the future – there surfaces a strange anxiety. The book is the precious material expression of a past emotion, or the chance of having one in years to come, and to get rid of it would bring the risk of a serious sense of loss. Whereas a collector frets obsessively about the books he does not yet possess, the fanatical reader worries about no longer owning those books – traces of his past or hopes for the future – which he has read once and may read again some day

But what lies behind this disturbing "reading fever"? The primal scene – of which naturally I have no memory – no doubt lies in that magical moment when one learns to read, and the infinite horizon that opens up when you decipher something written down. I spent my childhood reading everything that came to hand – books, yes, but also posters, advertisements, notices, newspaper cuttings, and during meals I would read cereal packets or bottle labels until I became expert on which companies were "by appointment to Her Majesty" or had received medals from various gastronomic competitions or exhibitions. An inextinguishable curiosity drove me to find out what lay behind the words and phrases, and the unknown reality on to which I had stumbled ("I should like you to be amazed not only by what you are reading, but by the miracle that it should be readable at all" – Vladimir Nabokov, *Pale Fire*). The fanatical reader is not only anxious, he or she is curious. And surely human curiosity – condemned as it was by certain Fathers of the Church as being of no purpose since the coming of Christ, and even prohibited, since we now have the Gospels – is one of the determining factors of all our actions? A capital element in the search for knowledge, in scientific discoveries or technological progress, the essential force behind human endeavour. And curiosity has no end: it is without limits. It feeds on itself, is never satisfied with what it finds, but must always press on, exhausting itself only with our dying breath. I read somewhere that a man sentenced to death during the revolutionary Terror read a book in the tumbril taking him to the scaffold, and turned down the page he had reached before climbing up to the guillotine. In Victor Hugo's play *Marion Delorme*, the king asks: "What is your reason for living?" and L'Angely replies "Curiosity." And reading expands indefinitely our perforce limited experience of reality, giving us access to distant ages, foreign customs, hearts and minds, human motivations, and everything else. How can you stop, once you have found the doorway offering the chance of escape from an inevitably constricted environment? Liberty was within arm's reach, so all I had to do was read and read, more and more, hoping to escape my individual destiny. Then I had only to add to this boundless curiosity a certain methodical tendency, which drove me to read all the works of a given writer, then all the books on him or her, then to move on to another writer, or all the books written on a certain subject, or the literature of a certain period, or country, and to wish as I went along to keep the books I had read, adding new ones that might be connected to them, gradually acquiring more topics I was interested in – and there I was – a bibliomaniac reader.

After that, a strange relationship becomes established between the bibliomaniac and his (or her) thousands of books. The same relation as between a gardener and an invasive climbing plant: the plant grows all by itself, in a manner invisible to the naked eye, but at a rate of progress that is measurable after a few weeks. The gardener, unless he is willing to chop it down, can only indicate the direction he wants it to take. In just the same way, prolific libraries take on an independent existence, and become living things. ("To build up a library is to create a life. It is never merely a random collection of books" – *The Paper House*.) We may have chosen its themes, and the general pathways along which it will develop, but we can only stand and watch as it invades all the walls of the room, climbs to the ceiling, annexes the other rooms one by one, expelling anything that gets in the way. It eliminates pictures hanging on the walls, or ornaments that obstruct its advance; it moves on with its necessary but cumbersome acolytes – stools and ladders – and forces its owner into constant reorganization, since its progress is not linear and calls for ever new kinds of division. At the same time, it is undeniably the reflection, the twin image of its master. To anyone with the insight to decode it, the fundamental character of the librarian will emerge as one's eye travels along the bookshelves. Indeed no library of any size is like another, none has the same personality.

3

ORGANIZING THE BOOKSHELVES

Only those who have done it know how great is the labour
of moving and arranging several thousand volumes. At the
present moment, I own about five thousand volumes and
they are dearer to me even than the horses, which are going,
or than the wine in my cellar, which is very apt to go,
and upon which I also pride myself.
ANTHONY TROLLOPE, *An Autobiography*

Any person who owns several tens of thousands of books is
faced with an inescapable problem: their classification. For if the
comfortable chaos of a few hundred books does not prevent their
owner (and their owner alone!) from finding his or her way around
them, the ordering of ten or twenty thousand books requires one
to have a retrieval system. In fact, that is usually the drift of the
second question invariably put by the "innocent" visitor – the first
one being: "And have you read them all?" A "fellow conspirator"
on the other hand, the moment I leave the room, will look over
the shelves, trying to work out the principle, and when I come
back in, will check – with not a little pride – whether his or her
hypothesis is correct. But even before that, comes the problem of

their physical accommodation. For books, unlike foodstuffs or other articles, can't just sit in cardboard boxes or live in piles. These are no more than temporary solutions, which make it impossible to use them. If they are going to be read, they have to be arranged on shelves in a way that makes them retrievable. And bookshelves take up space, even if whole rooms – not just their walls – can be devoted to them, as in university libraries. The ideal, of course, would be to have a purpose-built library, adapted to the books one owns, and reflecting the image one has of it. Alberto Manguel, for instance, had the barn of a former priest's house in Poitou specially organized. The photograph in the French edition of *The Library at Night* bears a disturbing resemblance to the library of the Colegio Nacional of Buenos Aires, which is pictured below it. You sense here a long-cherished dream being realized. To emulate Boulard, whom I mentioned earlier, one might buy several buildings in Paris – but that would require a great deal of money. A certain poet in Montmartre, finding that his original flat had become crammed with books, turned it into his office-cum-library, and moved his home across the street. We can be sure of one thing: the vast personal libraries one might have found in Paris in past days have become unattainable for the scholar or professor who does not have, in a now-outdated expression, "private means". Georges Dumézil would not today be able to luxuriate in his chaotic collection of printed works in the rue Notre-Dame-des-Champs. The same is true of all major capitals. I have a cutting from the "Culture" supplement of *The New York Times* dated 5 September, 1985 and entitled "The Problem of Living with Too Many Books" – note that *too many* books", rather than "a lot of books". The article mentions several real-life examples: the writer M. L. Aronson, who stored 7500 volumes in an apartment on the Upper West Side; Richard Kostelanetz, an author and artist who had 10,000 books in a loft in Soho; the journalist James Dantziger, who kept 1000 books in a small studio flat on Fifth Avenue. The article was accompanied by two "practical" inserts, in the usual spirit of the American press, informing readers about solutions for arranging their interiors, complete with materials and systems for shelving books, and providing prices, addresses and telephone numbers of stores where they could buy them.

But bibliomaniacs, like certain social classes, are doomed to abandon the inner cities, and move out to suburbs better adapted to their income and the kind of space they need. Another solution is to live in town and keep one's library in a second home, more or less devoted to it. But living hundreds of kilometres from one's books requires a whole material – and mental – reorganization of one's life.

Before long, in any case, this kind of problem will probably be of interest only to a few people. Downloading from the internet, looking up books on websites – and the possibility, at any hour of the day or night, and from any corner of the globe, of finding an out-of-print book through an online network of second-hand dealers – is surely on the way to making this dilemma redundant. And with ever greater specialization of fields of research, we are

surely going to see the disappearance, or at any rate the dim-
inution, of large-scale personal libraries of a general character.
Bibliophiles will still keep their collections, and libraries devoted to
precise topics will survive, but we may be pretty sure that vast and
unwieldy personal collections of a few tens of thousands of books
are likely to disappear, taking their phantoms with them. This little
book is being written from a continent which is about to be lost
for ever.

Once you have decided how to house the books, there is the
vast and inexhaustible subject of how to classify them.

Georges Perec long ago made a brave attempt at listing the
possible methods of classifying one's books:

> alphabetically
> by continent or country
> by colour
> by date of acquisition
> by date of publication
> by size
> by genre
> by literary period
> by language
> by frequency of consultation
> by binding
> by series

But Perec was well aware that "none of these choices is satisfactory on its own", and that "in practice, every library is arranged using a combination of these methods". Any rule can apply only if it allows for exceptions, determined by choice or necessity from the subjective options of the owner. Not a few writers seem to take malicious pleasure in thwarting any principle of classification. And there are countless "unclassifiable" items. The problem is not how to observe a self-imposed rule in order to justify its validity, but how to retrieve a book when you need it. Years afterwards. So the exceptions have to obey a sufficiently solid logical process to be reconstituted later, defying the passage of time.

Take classification by language for example. Would you put Nabokov's books written in three different languages – Russian, French and English – under those headings, or should you put them all together? And if so, which language would you choose? Russian was his mother tongue, but his most significant books were probably the ones he wrote in English. Should you shelve Spanish authors alongside those of Latin America? The language may be the same, or almost, but the literatures are very different. The same problem arises for Portugal and Brazil, and one could add writers from former Portuguese colonies (Angola and Mozambique) who write in Portuguese. What about minority languages, for instance those of the Baltic States? There are not enough translations available for each to have a separate section. But if not, then does one opt for a geographical criterion, putting them together, or by linguistic coherence (Lithuanian and Latvian are Indo-European languages, but Estonian is Finno-Ugrian). Or for convenience do they have to stay where they were, assimilated to the ex-Soviet Union?

Then again, if you choose countries, what do you do with autonomous regions? Since Barcelona is now the centre of linguistic nationalism, should I keep my Catalan books on the Spanish shelves? Not to speak (since it is an even more explosive subject) of books by Basque authors. And it is only for the sake of completeness that I even mention the former Soviet Union, which I have given up trying to rationalize. Whether it is by languages or countries, the fate of books translated out of Uzbek or Tajik, which Gallimard used to publish in its "Soviet Literature" collection, whose general editor was the eclectic (within Party lines!) Louis Aragon, is not now easy to resolve. So in my cowardly way, I have left this section under its Soviet arrangement, although it contains at least two Kazakh authors (Mukhtar Auezov and Abdejamil Nurpessov) to whom, if I had been more conscientious, I ought to have added the Tajik Sadriddin Ayni, or the Ukrainian Yuri Ianovski. From the point of view of classification, the ex-Soviet empire had some advantages! Another thorny problem was the former Yugoslavia. While the works of Ivo Andrič, Nobel prize winner in 1961, were traditionally described as being translated from the "Serbo-Croat", the last two to appear in French – *Signes au bord du Chemin* (Signs along the road), 1997, and *Contes au fil du temps* (Tales down the years), 2005, are translated "from the Serbian". The publishers, L'Âge d'homme, had previously indicated that *Au temps d'Anika* (Anika's time) and *La soif et autres nouvelles* (Thirst and other stories) had been written originally in Serbo-Croat.

Or take another writer, and potential Nobel candidate from the same generation as Andrič, Miroslav Krleza – whose name has sometimes been written in France as "Karleja", to help French people pronounce it, a fruitless attempt at literary marketing since this great writer remains unknown there. He was in some cases said to be translated from "Serbo-Croat", as in the Calmann-Lévy publications of *The Return of Philip Latinowicz*, 1957, and *The Banquet in Blitva*, 1964; and in others as from "Croatian", as in the Calmann-Lévy edition of *Mars, dieu croate* (Mars, a Croatian god), 1971, and *Les Ballades de Petritsa Kerempuh* (Ballads of Petritsa Kerempuh), Publications orientalistes de France, 1975. In the last example, the title page tells us that it was in fact translated from Kaikavian, a dialect from northern Croatia. *L'Enterrement à Theresienbourg* (Burial at Theresienburg), published by Minuit in 1957, was even cited as being translated by Antun Polanscak out of something called "Yugoslavian" – a hitherto unknown language that has definitely disappeared. So in this case too, I have swept under the carpet the political upheavals following the collapse of the Soviet empire and kept my Yugoslav section (an exception to my classification by language), mixing up Serbs and Croats with Slovenian and Bosnian writers. The Montenegrins and Macedonians do not figure here, but that is because after a careful inspection of the section, I am obliged to admit, to my embarrassment, that my library contains no books translated from these two languages.

Of course, I have no diplomatic dilemmas to face in my own home, but I can imagine the anxiety of cataloguers in public libraries when they have to face situations like this.

To return to Perec's list, one could try straightforward "alphabetical order". But what is one to do with collective or anonymous works, or those written by two authors? Do you shelve the book under Fruttero or Lucentini? Boileau or Narcejac? Zerner or Rosen? Bourdieu or Passeron?[1]

And in any case, that is to ignore exotic scripts like Mandarin, where the rules for transcription have been modified over time. If we choose instead continent or country, the first is too vast a category, while the second, as we have just noted, poses its own problems. Shelving by colour was the system adopted by Valery Larbaud, a method he devised at the end of his life, so as to be able to spot the original languages of the books in his library. The problem there was that it would mean having everything rebound or covered, and there are more languages than there are easily-distinguishable colours. Shelving "by date of acquisition" would mean a meticulous set of records, and you would have had to establish the system from the very start, in other words at a time when it was impossible to anticipate the catastrophe to come. (At

[1] Translator's note: The Italian writers Carlo Fruttero and Franco Lucentini published many books jointly, often signing as F & L; Pierre Boileau and Thomas Narcejac did the same in France; Henri Zerner and Charles Rosen co-authored some works on art history, and Pierre Bourdieu and Jean-Claude Passeron jointly wrote several sociological studies.

the age of eighteen, one does not take a conscious decision to be burdened with 40,000 books one day in the future.) After that, it is too late to be able to follow the rule reliably. "Classification by size" means that by definition there are only exceptions. "By date of publication" means choosing between the date of the first edition – not always easy to establish – and that of the copy you happen to own. And what about translations? "By genre" is a category very difficult to stick to: if you interpret it too widely it becomes useless, and if you employ it too narrowly, it leads to Byzantine discussions. Sorting books "by literary period" will not work internationally: literary periods are often quite independent of one another, depending on country or language, and the definition is never clear-cut. "By frequency of consultation" will apply only to a select number of books and will change over time too. Classifying "by binding" is an option open only to bibliophiles. "By series" leaves out the countless books that come in no series at all.

So the solution I propose – and it's stupid even to do so, since all owners of huge libraries have already chosen how to classify them, and the others won't bother – is to combine several of these orders, allowing some latitude to one's own rules. A principle you could extend, of course, to life in general.

Human reality sometimes intrudes strangely into the principles of classification. Christian Galantaris quotes the following extract from the rules of an English library of 1863: "The perfect mistress of a household will see to it that the works of male and female authors are decently separated and placed on different shelves. Unless the parties are married to one another, their proximity is not to be tolerated". This confirms the view that the principle of ordering one's books may be a warning sign of the owner's mental disorder – in the case above, that of Victorian society as a whole. In the case of the hero of *The Paper House*, the principle applied is that of "affective relationships". Carlos Bauer does indeed try to avoid two authors who dislike each other finding themselves neighbours on his bookshelves:

> ... for example, it was unthinkable to put a book by Borges
> next to one by García Lorca, whom the Argentine writer
> once described as "a professional Andalusian". And given
> the dreadful accusations of plagiarism between the two of
> them, he could not put something by Shakespeare next to
> a work by Marlowe, even though this meant not respect-
> ing the volume numbers of the series in his collection
> [Elizabethan drama]. Nor of course could he place a book
> by Martin Amis next to one by Julian Barnes, after the two
> friends had fallen out, or Vargas Llosa alongside García
> Márquez.

On the other hand, he also puts together some curious bedfellows, a course which he likes to justify ("Dostoevsky ended up closer to Roberto Arlt than he did to Tolstoy. And again: Hegel, Victor Hugo and Sarmiento deserve to be closer together than Paco Espínola, Benedetti and Felisberto Hernández"). In the same way, a certain

Henri Quentin-Bauhart (mentioned by Galantaris) thought of "marrying" various books to each other: by that he meant he would bring together in his library two books equally cherished. For example, he brought together a 1532 edition of Clément Marot with a Louise Labbé of 1555 and so on. We do not know what effect on this arrangement would have been produced by the recent revelation that Louise Lab[b]é may never have existed – that perhaps "her" works were written by a group of poets from Lyon (Maurice Scève, Olivier de Magny, Jacques Pelletier du Mans and others) who all frequented the printing house of Jean de Tournes, as postulated by Mireille Huchon in *Louise Labé, une créature de papier* (Louise Labé, a paper creation). Perhaps Labbé would no longer have been judged worthy to be placed next to Marot. As for Alberto Ruy Sanchez, author of *Mogador: the Names of the Air*, he crossed a further threshold regarding the potential intimacy between two books on a shelf: "It is said that if at night, in certain very pleasant sections of the Mogador library, two books which have affinities with one another are placed together, next morning one will find three of them …"

While on the subject of ultra-subjective ways of classifying books, one should not omit to mention the great art historian Aby Warburg, who also had some serious psychological problems. The son of a wealthy Hamburg banker, he had, the story goes, sold to his brother Max his birthright as eldest son to run the family bank, in return for unlimited credit with which to buy books for the whole of his lifetime. That led to the 100,000 volumes of the

Warburg Institute, now housed in London, which has occupied such an important place in the history of art in the twentieth century. Originally private, Aby Warburg's library evolved continually, according to its owner's mental itinerary and his principle of the "law of good neighbourliness". His chief concern was the "survival of the ancient" and Fritz Saxl, who was the first librarian of the collection, himself testified that, "The arrangement of books on the shelves was disconcerting: anyone walking in would have found it odd, to say the least, that Warburg wore himself out moving them around all the time". Ernst Cassirer, who had worked there, said at Warburg's funeral in 1929: "From the sequence of books there emerged, in ever clearer fashion, a series of images, themes and original ideas. And behind their complexity, I eventually came to see taking shape the clear and dominating figure of the man who had built up this library, and his personality as a researcher destined to have a far-reaching influence."

More modestly, I can now offer a precise example of classification, the one I know best: my own. My library is arranged by genre and sub-genre, with books being placed alphabetically within sections. There are three main categories: literature; non-fiction (a terrible Anglicism, which unfortunately does not have a French equivalent); and the arts.

Literature is subdivided into languages, but the Catalans are in the Spanish section, Frédéric Mistral (who wrote in Provençal) is in the French section, and if the Scandinavian section contains books translated from Icelandic, Danish, Swedish, Norwegian and even

Norse, it also contains Finnish literature which, strictly speaking, ought to be shelved with Hungarian, or – why not? – with Estonian. But this would have been to infringe a kind of literary taboo, comparable, I must admit, to the very outdated theory of climate, and which would in any case have faced me with another problem: Finnish authors who write in Swedish. So the language of expression would have trumped the cultural community, something I refused to allow to happen. (The owner of a large library quickly becomes a kind of autocrat, going so far as to interfere even with other people's books. Visiting a colleague, I own up to having surreptitiously rearranged different volumes of a work which have got out of order, or turned a book round if it is lying on its side so that its title is upside down!) And I confess I have not yet found an acceptable solution for Frisian – for example, I have a copy of *Tjerne le Frisian* by Gysbert Japicx, translated into French by Henk Zwier. The translator tells us that Frisian is a language belonging to the Germanic group, very close to Old English, and that it is mostly spoken in the northern Netherlands. The book was oddly enough in the Scandinavian section when I finally traced it, but I am not sure I will put it back there! And I should perhaps say that I have an entire subsection bringing together, without any distinction of language of origin, all my crime novels and thrillers.

My non-fiction section has two main divisions, which are far from rigorous: abstract (consisting of philosophy, theology, history of religions, science, psychoanalysis, psychology, literary criticism, linguistics, literary history) and concrete (history, politics, anthropology, autobiography, biography, and documents). I know, I know, this raises subtle questions of definition. Above all, there is the dilemma posed by authors both of theoretical works and of other books which take us closer to the material world. Should I put Norbert Elias's *What is Sociology?* next to his more historical works? Should Paul Veyne's *Comment on écrit l'histoire* (Writing history) be next to his studies of sexuality and euertegism (gift-giving) in ancient Rome?

The arts section is perforce much subdivided: music, cinema, photography, painting and drawing, architecture, exhibition catalogues and – for reasons of size – art history, criticism and aesthetics. These subdivisions are further divided: painting is by school (French, Italian, Flemish, German, etc.), the catalogues are split between museum catalogues by country, one-man shows, and thematic exhibitions (*Art in Medieval France; Pictures within Pictures; Melancholy* – and these are shelved chronologically). There is a whole bookcase containing art books that do not fall into any category. I will stop at this point, to spare the reader, but I could go on for ever, pointing out exceptions or tricky cases – does Picasso count as French or Spanish? Modigliani as Italian or French? Giacometti as Swiss? Do I treat Bernini as a painter or a sculptor (oh yes, sculpture is another sub-section) – or, indeed, as an architect? And what am I to do with Michelangelo?

Finally, there is a large wall behind my worktable where I have shelved all my reference works – dictionaries of all kinds, lexicons (philosophical, psychoanalytic, gastronomy, etc.). But the

1970 edition of the *Encyclopedia Universalis* has recently had to be moved to a nearby room, for reasons of space (I had to make some room for works on French painting because there has been such a rapid expansion recently in the activities of museums and art publishers).

This apparently impeccable ordering is in fact unsettled by many individual cases that present knotty problems – these have been resolved in a particular way but might equally well have been decided otherwise – as well as by a number of perhaps more logical exceptions. It was very tempting to put all my Pléiade editions (a uniform series, leather-bound and on bible paper, published by Gallimard) in a special bookcase suited to their size, but some of them are in fact shelved with the other works by a given author. Some complete collections have interrupted the purely alphabetical order of their section. Periodicals are shelved in a special bookcase, but these too are sometimes placed by genre. Volumes in a collection called Les Cahiers de l'Herne, which has a particular shape, are in theory placed together, but since I have run out of space, some of them are with the other books by the author in question.

I can only find my way around because I have personally placed each book in its position, one by one, down the years, and any changes were thought about long enough at the time to enable me to remember them. But all this doesn't prevent me from sometimes searching high and low when trying to find, say, a book translated from Romanian or Dutch (including Flemish), while the

Walloons are in the French section. (The hypothetical partition of Belgium, so often talked about, has become fact in my library.) These sections are too specific to be easily included with others, but small enough to be moved from time to time, and too limited in number to be picked out at a glance. Sometimes I spend time looking for a book for which the logical place has been overtaken by events. Or failing to find a book that I know I have somewhere. Have I mis-shelved it or is it lost? I cannot always answer that question, or else it is answered too late, when I have already bought another copy. When that happens, should I keep both of them? And if not, then which one?

4

THE PRACTICE OF READING

To own books without reading them is like
having a painting of a bowl of fruit.

DIOGENES

"And have you read all of them?" No, of course not! Or maybe not.
Actually, I don't know. It's complicated. There are some books I
have read and then forgotten (quite a lot of those) and some which
I have only flicked through but which I remember. So I may not
have read them all, but I have turned their pages, sniffed them,
handled them physically. After that, the book might take one of
three possible directions (I'm speaking now of books I have chosen
or acquired, that is in some way selected, rather than of books
received). They may be read immediately, or pretty soon; they may
be put off for reading later – and that could mean weeks, months
and even years, if circumstances are particularly unfavourable, or
the number of incoming books is too great – in what I call my "to
read" pile. Or they may go straight on to the shelf. Even those
books have been "read" in a sense: they are classified somewhere in
my mind, as they are in my library. They will serve their turn one
day, I don't know when or what for just now, but they're not sitting

there by chance. Books that deserve a mention here are those we have read, but did not appreciate, or those we will never get along with because, written by geniuses though they might have been, they don't say anything to us; books that need a second reading to be absorbed properly; books we might want to re-read purely for pleasure; and ones we will probably never open again but don't want to lose sight of; finally there are all those authors whose complete works we promise ourselves we will tackle one day, and others we should like to discover. And so on. ("The truth is that a library, whatever its size, does not need to have been read cover to cover to serve a useful purpose" – Alberto Manguel.) Seneca, however, considered that the vast numbers of scrolls in the library at Alexandria amounted to so many "dining-room decorations".

"Then you must have some method for fast reading?" Yes, I do, of course, but only one. For the last fifty years I have spent a great deal of my time reading all kinds of books, in all kinds of circumstances and for all sorts of purposes. And as with any activity which has become familiar, whether manual, artistic or sporting, you do acquire a kind of special relationship with the object in question, in this case the printed word. ("Years of work are required before the cerebral mechanisms for reading, if regularly oiled, finally become unconscious" – Stanislas Dehaene.) The important thing is not so much to read fast, as to read each book at the speed it deserves. It is as regrettable to spend too much time on some books as it is to read others too quickly. There are books you know well, just from flicking through them, others you only grasp at second or third reading, and others again which will last you a lifetime. A detective novel can be read in a few hours, but to prepare a lecture on the few pages of *The Waste Land* demands several days. The most extreme imbalance between the time one can spend on a text and its actual length might be to write an essay on Apollinaire's famous one-line poem: "Et l'unique cordeau des trompettes marines" ("And the single string of the tromba marina"). Writing a review of a book which has just been published means – at least in my case – reading it twice: once to discover the book as an innocent reader, and once more to put some order into one's impressions and ideas. And in the end, you forget a great deal of what you have read. In *How to Talk about Books You Haven't Read*, Pierre Bayard has written brilliantly about how all of us can find ourselves talking knowledgeably about books we have only heard about. A bit too brilliantly indeed, since the mass of assimilated reading matter that can be glimpsed behind his argument flagrantly contradicts what he says! He also remarks on the oblivion into which most of the books we *have* read will fall. "In the first place, it is hard to be quite sure if one has read a book or not, since reading is such a transitory thing." Even when the book really has been read and absorbed well enough to have a specific place in our minds, what we recall is often a memory of the emotion we felt while reading it, rather than anything precise about its contents. (Years later, you give this title as a gift to someone because you remember having loved it long ago, but you are quite unable to discuss it with the recipient because the details have disappeared beyond recall.)

In *Reading in the Brain*, Stanislas Dehaene shows how singular an event the coming of reading was for human evolution. It is a fairly recent activity for the human brain: the Babylonian invention of writing occurred about 5400 years ago, and the alphabet was created about 3800 years ago – too recently, in other words, for our genome to have time to alter to develop brain circuits adapted to reading. ("How was it that the cerebral architecture of a strange two-legged primate, which became a hunter-gatherer, adjusted so minutely in a few thousand years to the difficulties raised by recognising writing?" – Stanislas Dehaene.) This faculty, which to the individual feels like magic is, therefore, also an improbable event in the story of human evolution and one of the most surprising aspects of brain function. Reading, which started originally as a way of receiving information (probably no more than tabulated accounts for goods, trade and transactions), made it possible to move on to noting less obviously instrumental thought processes, then to transmitting them over distances – and by leaving them for future generations to find, encouraged the accumulation and constant enrichment of written artefacts. With writing, and therefore reading, humanity did not just make a quantitative cultural leap, it completely changed the scale of human thought. Humans became complex thinking beings. ("*Homo sapiens* is the only primate capable of pedagogy, in the sense that this species alone can pay attention to the knowledge and mental state of others for teaching purposes. Not only do we actively transmit the cultural objects we deem useful but – and this is particularly noticeable in the case of writing – we deliberately perfect them. So over five thousand years ago, the first scribes discovered a hidden capacity of the human brain, that of learning to transmit language through the eyes" – Stanislas Dehaene.)

It is hardly surprising that reading should be experienced as a unique activity, and in my own case, there is always the euphoria of being able to put a reality behind the name of an author or the title of a book. ("I read without selecting, just to get in touch" – Walter Benjamin.) Until it has been read, a book is, at worst, a jumble of signs on the page, at best a vague, perhaps false image, arising from what one has heard about it. To pick up a book in your hands, and discover what it really contains is like conferring flesh and blood, in other words a density and thickness, that it will never lose again, to what was previously just a word. For example, to someone who has not read Knut Hamsun's novel, *Pan*, that word will just be a set of three letters, usually denoting one of the divinities of nature. Once you have read the book, it will be forever linked to the scents and sounds of the forest behind the cabin in Nordland where Lieutenant Thomas Glahn lived with his dog Aesop, and where Edvarda, the daughter of the trader Mack, would sometimes come to find him; and to the two wild duck feathers which the lieutenant "with the blazing eyes of a wild beast" would receive two years later, folded into a sheet of paper embossed with a coat of arms. Or, to change countries, what would someone who has not read them make of the names of Kafū Nagai (1879–1959), the melancholy and sarcastic poet of the venomous charms of *La Sumida* (The [river] Sumida), set in the red-light district of Tokyo, or Osamu Dazai (1909–1948), the tubercular and desperate author of *Setting Sun* and *No Longer Human*? Once they have been discovered, the works of these two writers will remain indelibly imprinted on the mind of the reader.

Every time you open a book for the first time, there is something akin to safe-breaking about it. Yes, that's exactly it: the frantic reader is like a burglar who has spent hours and hours digging a tunnel to enter the strongroom of a bank. He emerges face to face with hundreds of strongboxes, all identical, and opens them one by one. And each time the box is opened, it loses its anonymity and becomes unique: one is filled with paintings, another with bundles of banknotes, a third with jewels or letters tied in ribbon, engravings, objects of no value at all, silverware, photos, gold sovereigns, dried flowers, files of paper, crystal glasses, or children's toys – and so on. There is something intoxicating about opening a new one, finding its contents and feeling overjoyed that in a trice one is no longer in front of a set of boxes, but in the presence of the riches and the wretched banalities that make up human existence.

Just imagine a man who has all day, and if he feels like it, all night too. And the money to buy every book he wants. There are no limits. He is at the mercy of his passion. And

> what is it that passion most wants? If you will allow me an observation […] it wants to discover its own limit. But that's no easy matter. Brauer was a conqueror, more than a traveller (Carlos Dominguez, *The Paper House*).

Yes, undoubtedly, the compulsive reader is a conqueror. And he considers the acres of print offered to him as fully equal to those conquered by Alexander, Genghis Khan, Tamburlaine or Napoleon – and at least as fascinating – and in any case calling for less futile devastation, cruelty and bloodshed.

The title of a book you have read (conquered?) has nothing in common with what it represented before. The book will now pursue its own life in your memory. Often, it will fall into oblivion. But it also happens that it develops of its own accord: the plot transforms itself, the ending has nothing to do with the one written by the author, its length can be radically altered. It was with surprise that I noticed, on picking up Silvio D'Arzo's *House of Others* again, after many years, that it has only sixty-five pages, whereas in my memory it had acquired another hundred over time. And I would never have imagined that when I re-read *Anna Karenina* twenty years later, I would feel more touched by the lot of Alexey Alexandrovitch Karenin than I had been inflamed, on first reading, by the passionate feelings of the lovely Anna for Vronsky. Not to mention the books of which one wonders, second time round, how one could ever have liked them. I had this disagreeable sensation a few years ago, on taking up again a book by Paul

Morand – either *Ouvert la nuit* (*Open all Night*) or *L'Homme pressé* (*The man in a hurry*) or *Hécate et ses chiens* (*Hecate and Her Dogs*) – I have now forgotten which. His lively style had enchanted me at the age of twenty, but now I felt oozing from his prose – still admittedly brilliant – a social disdain, a feeling of haughty superiority, a pompous self-satisfaction, which I found intolerable. So all that is left to me now of Morand is his *Ode to Marcel Proust* ("A shade / rising from the smoke of your fumigations / your face and voice consumed by your night watches / Céleste with her gentle rigour drenches me in the dark marinade of your chamber / smelling of warm cork and the ashes in the grate"). Here he was speaking as a friendly witness – and the subject of the poem made Morand's later anti-Semitism a paradoxical absurdity.

"And how do you read your books? And where?" Anywhere, and in any position. I am at any rate very far from the refinement of Guarino, of whom Anthony Grafton tells us that he "liked to read a text while out in a boat, his book on his knees. This way he could enjoy the pleasures of reading simultaneously with the sight of the fields and vineyards". Seated, standing, walking – why not? But the ideal is to be lying down, as if the position allows the text to enter the body more easily. Reading has enabled me to shorten the longest journeys, not to notice the hours I have spent waiting in airports, and for two decades to put up with meetings as futile as they were interminable, but which I could not escape. There remain strongly fixed in my memory books so absorbing that they seemed to make time stand still: Lawrence Durrell's *Alexandria*

Quartet, which I read in May 1968, since "the events" permitted me to devote myself to them full-time; *War and Peace*, which I finished in the back of a car between Paris and Marseille; Musil's *The Man without Qualities*, which I read with wonder, while walking, one spring in the early 1970s, towards Caesar's tower on the road between Les Pinchinats and Aix-en-Provence; *The Spy Who Came in from the Cold*, which I began one afternoon and to continue reading which I cut short a dinner-party invitation, finishing it in the early hours of the morning; *Moby-Dick*, some pages of which I re-read on the whaling island of Nantucket, where I noticed on several letter-boxes the surname Coffin, which figures in Melville's novel. I am lucky enough to be able to read no matter how noisy it is around me, in crowds or even surrounded by conversations of no interest. I am capable of reading all day, and carrying on late into the night, and to find it restful after a busy day. Reading tires me out as little as it tires fish to swim or birds to fly. I sometimes have the impression that I have really only existed through reading, and I would hope to die, like Victor Segalen in the forest of Huelgoat, with a book in my hand.

I write on my books, in pencil, but also with felt pens or ball-points. In fact I find it impossible to read without something in my hand. This is no doubt a habit arising from years of correcting proofs: the book for me is more of a tool of the trade than an object to be respected. Like other people who have worked in publishing or printing, I can't stop myself from correcting typos, grammatical errors or misprints in the books I am reading (and when

I happen to know the publisher or the author, I feel obliged to send him or her the corrections to incorporate in any new edition, and I have appreciated the few people who have done the same for me). To write on a book helps my reading, but it also helps me to remember the book and to come back to it later. I can hold in mind for months the approximate visual image of the place in the book where the passage occurred that struck me: top or bottom of the page, left or right hand, beginning or end – or else I note at the end of the book the page numbers to which I will have to return.

The experience of living with thousands of books is not without its influence on the functioning of memory. My memory works best at being able to find quickly the book the information is in, rather than by loading itself with facts, dates and quotations which are sitting on my bookshelves. Of course that requires my memory, my bookshelves, and the order of the books on the shelves all to be in good working order. When I am away from my library, I often feel as though I am handicapped, as if I had been amputated of some vital limb. It can go beyond needing a simple piece of information: sometimes it has more to do with the emotion or the idea – and its exact formulation – that one was trying to recollect. Years later, thanks to my marginal notes or the passages I underlined on the first reading, the content of the book comes back to mind in a few seconds. ("… On my old copy of *The Critique of Pure Reason* are inscribed my underlinings from thirty years ago; the pencil markings are from one decade, the ballpoint marking from another. They carry the memory of my relationship to the book" – Umberto Eco.) Or Alberto Manguel again:

> I always write in my books. When I re-read them, most of the time I can't imagine why I thought a certain passage worth underlining, or what I meant by some marginal comment. Yesterday I came across a copy of Victor Segalen's *René Leys*, dated "Trieste 1978". I don't remember ever being in Trieste (*A Reading Diary*).

Charles Nodier devotes several pages to "bibliology" in his *Hommes célèbres qui ont signé ou annoté leurs livres* (Famous men who signed or annotated their books). He cites the case of a copy of the *Essays* given by Montaigne to Charron; several copies of *The Imitation of Christ* translated into verse by Corneille and offered to people as gifts; various works signed by Rousseau or Voltaire; and he claims himself to be the happy owner of an Aeschylus which once belonged to Racine, while his Euripides and Aristophanes came from the Royal Library.

The tens of thousands of books with their underlinings and marginalia, which have absorbed a large proportion of the money I have earned in my working life, are therefore now of no commercial value. That makes a kind of sense, since I have always considered them as a sort of mental and material extension of myself, destined to go out of existence when I do (symbolically that is, since to bury them, or even cremate them with me – an original approach and more elegant in any case than having oneself cremated or buried in the company of one's family, arms, horses and servants – would pose considerable practical problems).

5

WHERE DO THEY ALL COME FROM?

Reading a book by Cervantes, Flaubert, Schopenhauer,
Melville, Whitman, Stevenson or Spinoza is an experience
as powerful as travelling or falling in love.

JORGE LUIS BORGES

How did these books get into my library? By a combination of
chance, systematic curiosity, and impulses generated by conversations or reading.

When I consider the discoveries I made long ago, the trigger
might have been a mysterious title (*Steppenwolf* for instance – in
French, the title is *Le Loup des Steppes* [Wolf of the steppes] – before
I had any idea who Hermann Hesse was); or it might be the book's
jacket (*Lolita* in the 1971 paperback version, at a time when I had
never heard of Nabokov, but was very taken by the illustration on
the cover: a close-up of the nape of the neck of a girl with blonde
plaits, against an elegant green background). Or perhaps I might
have seen the film before reading the book (Visconti's *The Leopard*,
from the book by Lampedusa; *The Treasure of the Sierra Madre*, by
John Huston, from the book by B. Traven; *The Big Sleep*, by Howard
Hawks from Raymond Chandler's original; *The Lady with the Little*

Dog by Kheifetz from Chekhov's story). It might be an anecdote – in one case, an article by Gilles Lapouge, which related how he had left a copy of Hamsun's *Pan* on a park bench, only to find it again the following year, at a second-hand *bouquiniste*'s on the banks of the Seine. The article in question also had the bewitching attraction of evoking a "secret society" of admirers of Knut Hamsun. How could one resist the chance to join a secret society of readers!

My systematic acquisitions come firstly from habits I have acquired as an eternal autodidact. No, I don't set out to read all the paperbacks there are in alphabetical order, though I do like to take a look at anything generally thought worthy of note. But it also comes from wanting to read everything by an author I have come across by chance. Or else by following a chain of affinities between different authors – for example, Diderot's *Jacques le Fataliste* led me to *Tristram Shandy*, Arthur Rimbaud sent me to Germain Nouveau. Leonardo Sciascia to Luigi Pirandello, and Pirandello to Giovanni Verga. Or perhaps a book by a single author has encouraged me to try and discover a whole body of literature. Let me take the example of *Pan* again (I still have Lapouge's article in a cutting from *Le Figaro littéraire* from 1972 – with on the back an article by Bernard Pivot entitled "134 French novelists, including '43 yearlings' [first-timers]", predicting who would win the Prix Goncourt that year). That single book drew me first to read all the rest of Hamsun's books that had been translated into French, which was not easy, since at the time most of them were out of print. I took years to find *August*, the last on my list, and that was in the Bibliothèque

Nationale, the old one, in the rue de Richelieu, when the books I had ordered for work purposes were taking a long time to arrive. I will never forget the feeling that flooded through me as I at last held in my hands the book I had been chasing for years, when it arrived on a trolley in the great reading room, the Salle Labrouste. At last I was going to find out what had happened to the unpredictable Edvarda! Then I embarked on reading all the Scandinavian literature translated into French that I could lay hands on (Dagerman, Lagerkvist, Jonson, Martinson, Vesaas, Laxness, and many more) and I even wrote a very serious article on Hamsun's novels *Benoni* and *Rosa* entitled "Une bague et un coeur que l'on brise" (A ring and a broken heart) in *La Quinzaine Littéraire* in 1980. But that wasn't all. I note, while looking at my copy (P. J. Oswald Editions), that *Pan* was number four in a French collection entitled "La source de la liberté" or "La solution intégrale" (the publisher of which announced that "this collection will publish great poets who chose to express themselves in prose"), and that at the time, I explored the whole collection and discovered the following numbers: (1) Haniel Long's *The Marvellous Adventure of Cabeza de Vaca* followed by *Malinche*, prefaced by Henry Miller, with the subtitle *Stories translated from American English by F. J. Temple*; (2) Hermann Hesse, *Demian*, translated into French by Denise Riboni, and (3) Albert Cossery, *Les Hommes oubliés de dieu* (*Men God Forgot*).

So once again I found Hermann Hesse in my journey through books and, above all, discovered Cossery (this must have been the first time I came across his books, a detail I had forgotten). On checking, I find that the Cossery is still on the shelves, but not the Haniel Long, which I am nevertheless certain I have read (have I lost it, lent it imprudently, or shelved it wrongly?). Nor is the Hesse – on the other hand, I do have the 1974 Stock edition of this, in the same translation by Denise Riboni, only it has been "revised and completed by Bernadette Burn" and "prefaced by Marcel Schneider". After that, I read everything I could find by Cossery: *Les Fainéants dans la vallée fertile (The Lazy Ones); La Maison de la mort certaine (The House of Certain Death); Mendiants et Orgueilleux (If all Men were Beggars)*. I went to see whether I had shelved the Long under Miller, but no. However I did find Miller's *Time of the Assassins: a study of Rimbaud*, which was number six in the collection. And this informed me that number five was *Séraphita*, which I then duly found shelved with the rest of my Balzac. And I was indeed to re-publish Balzac's *La Théorie de la démarche* (Theory of walking) a few years later for Pandora editions in 1978. So starting from an article in *Le Figaro*, I have systematically read through Hamsun, explored Scandinavian literature, and acquired books from a particular collection, which in turn led me to other discoveries. I have only gone into so much detail over this example to indicate how infinite the ramifications of one's reading can be. One has only to imagine hundreds of cases like this, to end up with thousands of books on the shelves.

As the years go by of course, the field of discoveries shrinks, the continents are explored one after another, surveyed, mapped and sometimes even colonized, which does not prevent one from time to time discovering a lost tribe in a particularly inaccessible region – recently, I found the surprising and delicious *The Time Regulation Institute* by Ahmet Hamdi Tanpinar, which shed light for me on some gaps in my knowledge of Turkish literature, despite my early appreciation of Nazim Hikmet.

And finally there are all the conversations. Those foreign friends who affectionately deliver to you the greatest authors in their own literature – which are not always the ones you would have guessed from the translations available – the books about which they speak to you with a tremor in their voice that inspires you to seek them out for yourself, the books they recommend to you as a special part of themselves, re-editions published by discerning readers. For example, the collection *Fins de siècles* (Ends of centuries), published by Hubert Juin in the series 10-18 in the 1970s and 1980s, led me to discover Marcel Schwob, Jean de Tinan, Octave Mirbeau, or Hugues Rebell. And what about the chance encounters? The Goncourts' *Journal*, spotted on the bookshelves of Leonardo Sciascia in his modern flat in Palermo, and which, to my shame as a Frenchman, I had never read. *Spoon River* by Edgar Lee Masters, recommended to me by Louis Evrard during a dinner in the rue Lepic. William Kennedy's *Legs*, recommended to me by Jim Salter when I asked him to name the American novel that he most regretted had not yet been translated into French. Another writer is John Cowper Powys, described enthusiastically by Max-Pol Fouchet, one evening on the French TV book programme *Lecture pour tous* (Reading for all) or *Apostrophes* –

I've forgotten which now. I could go on. Don Marquis's *Archy and Mehitabel*; Anders Nygren's *Agape and Eros*, Mario Praz's *The Romantic Agony*; Yuri Kazakov; Silvio d'Arzo's *Casa d'altri* (The house of others); *Petersburg* by Andrey Bely; *The Art of Describing* by Svetlana Alpers; *Story of My Wife* by Milan Füst – and more. They are all linked to memories of people now dead, or with whom I have lost touch, and to whom I owe an immense debt. That's the way books get around.

And I haven't even started on bookshops. There has always been one in every town in which I have ever lived, some more memorable than others. (Oh yes! I remember Marie-Jeanne Apprin's Librairie de Provence, in Aix-en-Provence in the 1970s; Brahic's shop, also in Aix, at the top of the Cours Mirabeau; Madame Tchann's bookstore on the boulevard du Montparnasse in Paris – later replaced by a shop selling golfing accessories, which quickly folded.) Bookshops with their daily deliveries, laid out on the "new books" table – sometimes their owners even opening the boxes before your very eyes – or with their treasures forgotten on the shelves. Christian Thorel found a copy of the out-of-print *Dom Casmurro* by Machado de Assis in the tiny bookshop called *Ombre blanche* (White shadow) in its early days. Even more precious are the books recommended by a bookseller who is also a great reader, when he or she has a moment to escape the administrative preoccupations that take up most of their time. Bookstores often become informal meeting places, where at certain times of day you are almost sure to find someone to talk to. True bookshops –

Tschann has now moved to another spot on the boulevard Montparnasse, or Le Livre in Tours (where they sell more books published by Clémence Hiver than by Grasset!) – have replaced the circulating libraries of the nineteenth century or the literary cafés, where it was a ritual to foregather in the late afternoon to meet people of similar interests. Or on a different tack, I remember José Corti in his bookshop on the rue Médicis in the early 1980s, getting cross because I asked him if he still had the two volumes of André Monglond's *Préromantisme français,* (French pre-Romanticism) which had long been out of print. He calmed down, and we moved from confrontation to conversation. After checking, I find that I actually have Monglond's book in my library, but I have now completely forgotten how it got there. I do know I paid a lot of money for it – 400 francs – because I have another tic, which is to leave the prices in all the books I have bought second-hand. In this case it was on a thin piece of card with a notch in it, since it had been attached to the book's jacket in the shop window.

Reviewers and writers are another source of ideas. Would I have found my way to reading Joubert, Broch or Musil without reading Maurice Blanchot's *Le Livre à venir (The Book to Come)*? How would I ever have got to Ammianus Marcellinus, or re-read Grégoire de Tours without Auerbach's *Mimesis* (my copy is in the Gallimard collection, Tel, dated 1977)? Would I ever have gone back to Rousseau without Jean Starobinski's *Jean-Jacques Rousseau: la transparence et l'obstacle (Jean-Jacques Rousseau: transparency and obstruction)*? And among the many critics who have helped me to understand Proust better (Deleuze, Revel, Beckett, Poulet and more) there is the precious stylistic approach of Leo Spitzer (*Linguistics and Literary History: Essays in Stylistics*). These critics – and some others – were not satisfied simply to analyse the books, but went on to shed new light on them for readers already familiar with their contents, while at the same time persuading new readers to seek them out. As did some authors, such as Claude Simon, who used to speak so luminously of Proust, or Julien Gracq, whose *Lettrines* and *En lisant, en écrivant* (Reading, writing) conveyed the impression of having a friendly conversation, of remarkable interest, with someone who had read the same books as oneself.

One final curiosity: lists. I have spent a good deal of my time drawing up lists of books to read or re-read, or of the few indispensable books I would take to a desert island. I am not of course alone in this. Raymond Queneau once edited a book consisting of nothing but booklists, *Pour une bibliothèque idéale* (The ideal library), in which about sixty individuals, writers and others, named their favourite books. Those consulted were arranged alphabetically, from Raymond Abellio to Edmond Vermeil, by way of Gaston Bachelard, Paul Claudel, Georges Dumézil, Michel Leiris and Jean Rostand; the book ended with the hundred most mentioned titles. Well, I conscientiously put a line through the ones I had read (I can't remember when I did this), marking with a star those that were in my personal pantheon. There are nine titles there which appear not to have been read at all: the plays of Sophocles and Aristophanes (read since); *Discourse on Method* by Descartes; the plays of Marivaux, Tacitus's *Annals* and *Histories*, Marx's *Das Kapital*, Voltaire's *Correspondence*; the *Thousand and One Nights*; and *The Dark Night of the Soul* by St John of the Cross. I'm not sure I will ever get round to reading these.

Henry Miller ended *The Books in My Life* (I read this in the French edition, *Livres de ma vie*, published by Gallimard, 1957) with a list of "books read" – though how can one be sure? On the list of "books I still intend to read", he lists exactly thirty-four, which is not a great many for a man who was only sixty-six at the time, but then he does add a dozen authors whose complete works he means to read: Jean-Paul Richter, Novalis, Croce, Toynbee, Léon Bloy, and so on, which gave him more scope. Finally came a list of "friends whom I acquired through books" (there are 117 of these, accompanied by the name of the town and country where they were living at the time).

Talk about lists and you think of collections. I am really neither a collector nor a bibliophile, but I do have one pathological habit: I hate having incomplete series. The itch starts if I happen to have acquired a few books in a certain collection: let's say the Cahiers de l'Herne, starting with a one-volume reprint of titles by Céline in 1972; the photographic albums accompanying Pléiade editions, which I have collected since I bought the one on Apollinaire published in 1971; a few books from "A la promenade" (Stock, 1927 for the first series and 1946 for the second, edited by Marcel Arland), a foray suggested to me by André Mauge, the delicious translator into French of the works of Primo Levi; the series *Peintres vus par eux-mêmes et leurs contemporains* (Painters as seen by themselves and their contemporaries) published by Pierre Cailler; and there are others. Then what happens is that I feel impelled to buy more from the collection, until there remain only a few titles to make the series complete. But the search for these titles can take years and raise false hopes (a book appears in a second-hand catalogue, but when you chase it up, it has just been sold). In some rare cases, you draw a complete blank. After fruitless attempts over the years to obtain volume one of the *Van Gogh* in the Pierre Cailler series, since I already owned volume two, it turned out that it had never existed! The opposite is more likely; so the second volume of George Painter's biography of Chateaubriand – of which the first, *Les orages désirés* (*The Longed-for Tempests*), was published by Gallimard in a translation by Suzanne Nétillard, in 1979 – never appeared either, but that was not particularly regretted. The first volume was no more than a redundant paraphrase of Chateaubriand's *Mémoires d'outre-tombe* (*The Memoirs of Chateaubriand*) and must have failed to sell many copies, so the publisher was not inclined to take it any further.

The weirdest thing that can happen is that at the end of this kind of long search, a few weeks after finally tracking down the volume you were after, you come across another copy of the longed-for book – and at a better price, of course! This happened to me with the *Art of Chinese Landscape Painting* by Anil de Silva, the French edition of which was the last in the series of fifty books on "L'art dans le monde" (Art in the world) published by Albin Michel

69

between 1960 and 1977. It is very tempting on such occasions to buy the additional copy, although you no longer have any use for it, in homage to the years of the chase.

6

READING PICTURES

Libraries, like museums, are a refuge from old age,
sickness and death.

JEAN GRENIER

In my study, the bookshelves are all devoted to art history. On my right, when I am sitting at my desk, are normal-sized books in alphabetical order of author, from Laurie Schneider Adams, *The Methodologies of Art* (and this may be an example of a category mistake since Schneider is, on reflection, more likely to be the first part of a double surname, not a second first name, but it's too late now) to Ludovico Zorzi, *Représentation picturale et représentation théatrale* (Pictorial and theatrical representation). On my left are the big art books. They have ended up invading every wall, pushing out any posters, engravings or pictures, and have spilled over into the room next door, where I keep catalogues and thematic studies, as well as works on architecture, photography and all kinds of coffee-table books. Monographs are classified in alphabetical order and by school (French, Italian, German, and so on), to make it easier to find them. Thematic works are grouped according to links which are sometimes a bit wayward. So *Metropolitan Cats* by John P.

O'Neill and *Le Chat et la palette* (*The Painted Cat*) by Elisabeth Foucart-Walter and Pierre Rosenberg rub shoulders quite amicably with *Le Chien dans l'art* (*The Dog in Art*) by Robert Rosenblum. Books on Saint Sebastian or Mary Magdalen sit alongside a Rath Museum catalogue of an exhibition on Cleopatra and *La Calomnie d'Apelle* (The calumny of Apelles) by Jean-Michel Massing. But the location of *L'Art et le temps, regards sur la quatrième dimension* (Art and time: views of the fourth dimension), a collective work edited by Michel Baudson, or *Le Monde à l'envers* (The world upside down) by Frédéric Tristan could only be the result of an arbitrary decision. Not to mention learned journals, in a field where recent research is often communicated in a short article of a few pages. If I have a whole run of a periodical title, like the 158 numbers of *La Revue de l'art* (Art Review) that's straightforward enough, but what am I to do with one-off issues of the occasional journal like the number 5–6 of *Macula* or the three issues I happen to own of *La Part de l'oeil* (The eye's share)?

The art books are in my study for purely practical reasons in the first instance: it's the only room in the house that is not affected by damp, whatever the season. But there's another aspect: the visual pleasure to be found when working alone. These books often have an illustration on the spine, and the titles instantly bring other images to mind. So when I am sitting in front of my computer, I can read titles like *Mantegna and the Bridal Chamber*, *The strange case of Félix Vallotton*, *King René and his age*, *Oudry's Animals* or *De Staël: from line to colour*. I have only to see the name of an artist (Georges Seurat say, or Jacapo da Pontormo) to see a flow of images which spring to mind as soon as I read the few syllables making up the title: the name of an artist is pregnant with all his or her works. Books which are text-only do not always conjure up images, because words make the images more fleeting. Reading the title *Madame Bovary*, given the reader's freedom of imagination and the many extraordinary scenes in the novel, somehow does not offer the same wealth of visual image.

Anyone interested in art and who has collected books about it immediately encounters two problems. The first is financial. Art books cost on average three or four times as much as other books – sometimes far more. And they never come out in cheap paperback form. Then once they are out of print, it is unusual for them to be reprinted. So their price on the second-hand market can shoot up. You therefore regret not having bought them at the time, which encourages you not to make the same mistake again; consequently you end up buying a great many books, so as not to feel later that you missed the boat. There's no end to it. As for exhibition catalogues, by definition, they are practically never reprinted once the exhibition has closed. So just to give one example, I don't possess, for some long-forgotten reason, the catalogue of the exhibition *Paris-New York* which was in the Pompidou Centre in Paris in 1977. Yes, I do own an edition which Gallimard published in 1991, but that only makes things worse, because it's in a smaller format and the cover is plastic, so it spoils my set of this series of exhibitions (*Paris-Berlin, Paris-Moscow, Paris-Paris*). The trouble is that the original would now cost me at least 450 euros (the equivalent of 2,950 francs!): in other words, ten or twelve times the 250 or 300 francs it would have cost when it came out. So now, when an interesting exhibition opens, how can I hesitate about buying the catalogue? It could even be considered money-saving! The taste for art books requires the income of a bibliophile, whereas the true lovers of these books are often short of money.

The second problem is their size and shape – generally irregular – and it means you have to shelve them in rather haphazard fashion, which complicates any thematic arrangement. So my copy of the French version of *The Age of the Grand Tour* by Anthony Burgess and Francis Haskell is problematic, not only because it has two authors and because of its subject, but also because of its format which is, Italian-style, 34 centimetres by 48.5. Consequently, I am the only person who knows where to find it – on the bookcase reserved for odd formats, which therefore holds a completely heterogeneous selection of titles – and more importantly, *why* it will be there.

Why do I have all these picture books? The first explanation is personal and anecdotal, but deeper than it might first appear. When I was about thirteen or fourteen, I was treated to the ritual visit to Paris for a boy from the provinces. I conscientiously visited Napoleon's tomb in the Invalides, and the Place du Tertre in Montmartre, and climbed to the second storey of the Eiffel Tower – on foot to save the price of the lift (the worst bit was going down again!). I marvelled at the fountains in Versailles, and spent half a day in the Louvre. When I got home, all I had retained from the hours spent in the museum was the memory of one picture: the *Mona Lisa*. Mortified, I understood that without preparation, without apprenticeship, without reading, you don't see anything when you visit an art gallery. I discovered after that that if you read certain art historians, they would shed as much light on the past, with as much ingenuity, as much subtlety and colour as historians in other fields. I still thrill to remember the way Panofsky showed me the links between scholasticism and Gothic architecture, or Millard Meiss explained the influence of the Black Death of 1348 on painting in Florence and Siena. And if I turned to the artists, once I had overcome the difficulty of getting to see their works, there was as much enlightenment to be found about their lives and their deepest emotions as from writers. One had to *learn* how to read images – just as I had had to learn how to read words – to be able to gain profit from them. ("Hundreds of people can talk for one who can think, but thousands of people can think for one who can see" – John Ruskin.) After that it was simply a matter of travelling, talking to people, joining in conversations, and reading books.

All these books have several functions. The images may accompany a theoretical or historical text – a period in art history, an individual artist, studies by Jakob Burckhardt, Heinrich Wölfflin, Elie Faure, Charles Sterling, Henri Focillon or Francis Haskell. Or they may be the main reason for having the book: to be able to discover or rediscover a work of art without leaving home. Of course, the images don't really speak unless you have physically seen the original – an exhibition catalogue only truly comes to life when you have been in the presence of the works. But they also bring you all the images that are too far away or inaccessible, the ones you will never see, and for which the reproduction is the only way you can grasp them.

The problem is that here too there are no limits to one's curiosity. Images send you on to other images, artists to other artists, periods come one after another or echo each other, all with their cargo of art works. From prehistoric art to Land Art by way of Praxiteles, Roman wall paintings, the portraits of Fayoum, Romanesque frescoes, Fontainebleau School engravings, baroque ceilings, ukiyo-e woodcuts, the churches of Minas Gerais, nineteenth-century American still lifes, not to speak of all the most obvious and unavoidable schools, the universe of forms is infinite. And historical approaches are always being modified by new discoveries (through archaeology, or documents, or even the reappearance of works once believed lost). As for interpretations, however brilliant and convincing, they seem inevitably to be disputed sooner or later. Panofsky's brilliant reading (*Studies in Iconology*) of the mysterious *Venus and Cupid* in the National Gallery in London has been contested by Maurice Brock, and that reading will no doubt be demolished in its turn. But no matter! In art history, the interest of all these interpretations and theories is not that they should be definitive, but that they should be coherent and relevant enough to make us really look at a work, and by so doing, to have some chance of appropriating it for ourselves.

I cannot leave out the memory of those magical places which have sent shivers down my spine. Just to mention a few, purely autobiographical experiences, not the most famous, and confined to France: seeing *The Descent from the Cross* in the crypt of the church in Chaource; the Isenheim altarpiece in Colmar; the priory of Serrabone in the Pyrenees; the Romanesque frescoes of Tavant; the Apocalypse tapestry in Angers; Fouquet's *Pietà* in Nouans; the Gallic ex-votos in the Bargoin museum in Clermont-Ferrand; *Irene Tending St Sebastian* by Trophime Bigot in the museum in Bordeaux; Puy-en-Velay cathedral, one summer's day when the lower doors were open and the steps up to the nave became a well of light. The emotions I might have felt then naturally call for their extension through a presence of some kind in my library, and perhaps require to be better understood by acquiring a scholarly commentary.

Once again, my mania for collecting all the books in a series makes me buy books which are on subjects that don't necessarily interest me – until the day when … ah, now I need it! One of the most unusual collections on my shelves is the art historical series "Histoire de l'art" published by Julliard from 1962. This is unusual because of the personality of the general editor, Jean-François Revel, who is much better known for his writings on philosophy, literature and gastronomy, or for his journalism (he was at one time editor of *L'Express*, then a columnist for another weekly, *Le Point*), as well as current affairs debates and several best-sellers such as *Ni Marx ni Jésus* (*Without Marx or Jesus*) and *La Tentation totalitaire* (*The Totalitarian Temptation*). But his role in producing this art series is much less well known. Having discovered the subject during a long stay in Italy, when he made the acquaintance of André Fermigier and Jacob Bean (the future curator of the drawings and engravings department of the Metropolitan Museum in New York), and having met both Bernard Berenson and Roberto Longhi, on his return to France he made a proposal for the series to René Julliard, and then recruited authors, all of whom were specialists. But none of the books has the same format: the French translation of Anthony Blunt's *Artistic Theory in Italy* is twenty centimetres high, whereas the French edition of Max Friedlander's *From Van Eyck to Bruegel* stands at twenty-seven centimetres. Nor do they have the same appearance: they all have a paper jacket except Bernard Teyssèdre's *L'Histoire de l'art vue du Grand Siècle* (Art history as seen from the *grand siècle* – seventeenth-century France). Two of the jackets are illustrated – Emil Kaufmann's *Architecture in the Age of Reason* and *Philibert de l'Orme* by Anthony Blunt – but the others carry only typography. Four of them have the series colophon, the other five do not. The Kaufmann, the Friedlander, one of the Blunts (*Artistic Theory in Italy*), and Kenneth Clark's *Landscape into Art*, all give the name of the translator, but we are not told who translated Michael Levey's *Painting in Eighteenth-century Venice*, John Golding's *Cubism*; Gombrich's *The Story of Art*, or Blunt's *Philibert de l'Orme*. To publish these books, all of them significant, but appealing to a fairly limited readership, and many of which had been published elsewhere, and to do so without any conformity of presentation, was asking for trouble in a commercially difficult area. After these nine titles were published, the collection came to an end in 1965.

So for me, books have been a way of "seeing something" in painting, but they have done other things too. For instance, I was able to decode a Benetton advertising campaign for students in the Paris School of Political Science (Sciences-Po), using the analytical tools of art history, which applied very well. And it is not so difficult to understand why St Barbara is particularly honoured in the Brazilian mining region of Minas Gerais – one of the biggest cities there is named Santa Barbara after her – if you know about Christian iconography: she has always been the patron saint of miners, protecting them from the dangers of their work. When Panofsky paid a visit to Henri Focillon in the 1930s – or perhaps it was to his daughter Hélène and her husband Jurgis Baltrusaitis (I can't remember and nobody can tell me now) – they took him to Colombey-les-deux-Eglises, and he went off looking for the second church. I have just discovered from a recent book, *Relire Panofsky* (Re-reading Panofsky by Georges Didi-Huberman et al.) that his visit to Focillon in Maranville took place in August 1933. The story is told of Bernard Berenson, on learning that the Virgin Mary had appeared to Pope Pius XII, he immediately asked the first question that would occur to an art historian: "And in what style?"

7

REAL PEOPLE, FICTIONAL CHARACTERS

The best bacon omelettes I have eaten in my life
have been with Alexandre Dumas.
JACQUES LAURENT

Hundreds of thousands of people live in my library. Some are real, others are fictional. The real ones are the so-called imaginary characters in works of literature, the fictional ones are their authors. We know everything about the former, or at least as much as we are meant to know, everything that is written about a given character in a novel, a story or a poem in which he or she figures. This character has not grown any older since the author brought him or her into existence, and will remain the same for all eternity. When we hold in our hand the text or texts in which such a person appears, it feels as if we are in possession of everything the author wanted us to know about the character's acts, words and, sometimes, thoughts. The rest doesn't matter. Nothing is hidden from us. For us, a novel's characters are real. We may be free to imagine what we don't know about them, though we know quite well that these are just guesses. And we are free to interpret their words or their silences, but again these will just be interpretations. We know

quite a lot about Odysseus, Aeneas or Don Quixote, correspond-
ingly little about Homer, Virgil or Cervantes. Sometimes characters are even deprived of an author as if their creator had discreetly
slipped away. Who made up the first version of Don Juan? Who
invented Faust? And while we feel sure that Harpagon, Tartuffe or
Monsieur Jourdain undeniably exist, what do we know in the end
about a certain Jean-Baptiste Poquelin, whose stage name was
Molière? Not very much, not even whether he really wrote all the
plays attributed to him. Pierre Louÿs devoted his final years to
trying to establish that Molière's plays were in fact written by
Corneille – which is not as far-fetched as it might at first appear
according to Goujon and Lefrère. Hamlet is a great deal more
present to us than Shakespeare, about whom we have only a
few scraps of information. Without even going into the question
of whether he wrote the plays, no traces remain (apart from his
recorded marriage to Anne Hathaway and the births of the
children, Susanna and twins Judith and Hamnet) of his activity
during his early manhood, 1579 to 1588, the period Shakespeare
scholars call "the lost years". So we shouldn't assume too much.

It's even worse, in fact, when we think we *do* know the author.
And this despite our knowledge that we know little or nothing
even about our contemporaries. Every day one learns with
surprise from the newspapers that, for instance, a certain notori-
ously homophobic conservative member of parliament has been
arrested for soliciting in the men's lavatories of an airport, or that
a prominent advertising man has been accused by his daughters

of sexual abuse, that the helpful neighbour was really a dangerous psychopath, that the women's downhill ski champion turned out to be a man, or that a respectable accountant was actually embezzling thousands to finance his addiction to the gaming tables. And yet we carry on believing what we read in biographies. (Curiosity is too strong: I have masses of biographies in my library!) They are simply imaginary reconstructions based on the necessarily fragmentary elements left by someone now dead, whether long ago or in the recent past. And as for autobiography, it is no more than a pernicious variant of romantic fiction.

We may be lacking many elements in the life of Henri Beyle, but the features Stendhal gave his fictional alter ego, Henry Brulard, are undeniable. Whole chunks of the life of Benjamin Constant are lost to us for ever, but his *Adolphe* is sufficiently realistic to have tempted at least four writers to set out to write the novel from Ellénore's point of view: Gustave Planche, *Essai sur Adolphe* (Essay on Adolphe) of 1843; Sophie Gay, *Ellénore*, of 1844; Stanislas d'Otremont, *La Polonaise* (The Polish woman) of 1957; Eve Gonin, *Le Point de vue d'Ellénore* (Ellénore's point of view) of 1981. This is because literary figures are so real that writers borrow them from each other as they navigate from one book to the next (there are countless Don Juans and Wandering Jews). They can even come unexpectedly to life. Apparently Balzac on his death-bed called for Horace Bianchon, his fictional doctor in *La Comédie Humaine*. ("Yes, that's it! Bianchon's the man I need! If only Bianchon were here, he'd save me!") The story is probably quite untrue, but it does suggest that in the moment of dying Balzac was aware that his characters would survive his death.

We are so anxious to maintain the illusion that the author is a real person that we cannot be satisfied simply with an orphan work of literature. It took centuries to identify Gabriel-Joseph de Lavergne, vicomte de Guilleragues, the supposed author of *The Portuguese Letters* (1669): this book was published as "Lettres portugaises traduites en françois, A Paris Chez Claude Barbin, au Palais, sur le second perron de la Sainte Chapelle, MDCLXIX" ("Portuguese Letters, translated into French, available at Claude Barbin's, Paris Palais de Justice, second staircase, Sainte Chapelle"). As for *Madame Solario*, an English novel published anonymously in 1956 (and translated into French by R. Villoteu in 1985), the theories about its authorship are legion, the most far-fetched being that it was written by no less a person than Winston Churchill.[2]

Authors are just fictional people, about whom we have a few biographical elements, never enough to make them truly real people. Whereas the biography of a literary character, even if it is incomplete – and explicitly so – is perfectly reliable: it is whatever its creator decided. So are his or her acts and words. All the same, we readily refer to biographies, after reading them (or even without), and quote them as if they were authentic. Anecdotes and *bons mots* from historical persons – including writers – often turn out, when you check them, to be apocryphal or mythical.

2 See Bibliography. This book is today usually attributed to Gladys Huntington.

As for what happens to both fictional and real people, they all do the same things: both kinds fall in love, deceive each other, murder, feel guilt, steal, run away, betray, make things up, sacrifice themselves, are cowardly, go mad, take revenge and end up killing themselves; but once again, even in such specific actions, the invented characters are the most real. We are certain that Carlos and Maria Eduarda in *The Maias* by Eça de Queiros have been incestuous lovers – even if they do not realise it themselves. But we don't know what happened between Byron and Augusta, George Trakl and his sister Margarethe, Egon and Gert Schiele, who as teenagers repeated their parents' honeymoon voyage, or Erika and Klaus Mann. We know more about the motives that drove Paulina Pandolfini to murder Count Michele Cantarini on 28 August, 1880, thanks to Pierre-Jean Jouve's novel *Paulina 1880*, than we do about those of Louis Althusser when he killed his wife Hélène. We know that Zeno Cosini in Italo Svevo's *Confessions of Zeno* married Augusta, although he was in love with her sister Adelina, and why he did; but the real reason why Tolstoy proposed to Sofia Behrs, rather than to one of her sisters Tatiana or Liza, who both seem at different times to have attracted him, remains obscure; similarly Mozart, who was in love with Aloisa Weber, married her sister Constanza. What extravagant arrangement drove Pierre Louÿs to marry Louise de Heredia, the sister of his lover, Marie de Régnier, with the latter's consent? We will never know why certain writers (Herman Melville, Robert Frost, Hugo von Hoffmansthal, Thomas Mann) had a child who committed suicide; but the suicide of

Edgardo Limentani is completely understandable after the few hours that it takes to read Giorgio Bassani's *The Heron* – and a great deal more so than the suicides of Count Potocki, or Ernest Hemingway, or Cesare Pavese, about whom many commonplaces have been aired to explain an act which is never commonplace. Whether Pirandello, Scott Fitzgerald or T.S. Eliot had any responsibility for the mental illness of their wives, Antonietta, Zelda and Vivien, will always be a mystery: but the madness of Catharine Holly in *Suddenly Last Summer*, by Tennessee Williams, is undeniably prompted by her aunt, Mrs Venable. Was Gorky poisoned by Stalin? Was Zola assassinated by the anti Dreyfusards, or was he the accidental victim of carbon monoxide poisoning from his stove? We shall never know. Will we ever find out why Pushkin imprudently challenged the Baron d'Anthès to a duel? On the other hand, we are quite certain that Thérèse Raquin and her lover Laurent drowned Thérèse's husband, Camille; and we know that Count Serlon de Savigny, with his beautiful mistress, the fencing champion Hauteclaire Stassin, poisoned the count's wife, Delphine de Cantor, and lived happily ever after – in Jules Barbey d'Aurevilly's, "Le Bonheur dans le crime" (Happiness in crime), a story in *The She-Devils*. As for Sherlock Holmes, Pierre Bayard recently demonstrated convincingly, in *Sherlock Holmes was Wrong: reopening the Hound of the Baskervilles Affair*, that the detective was on completely the wrong track, and that Conan Doyle, in his inquiry into the mysterious deaths on Dartmoor, did not actually know what was going on. ("Literary characters are not, as is too often believed, paper creatures, but living beings who lead an autonomous existence within the texts and may even commit murders without their author realising it!") Finally, in the case of two historical persons, I am far more convinced of the authenticity of Alexandre Dumas's Henri III in *Chicot the Jester* and *The Forty-five Guardsmen* than by the one described by many historians, including Michelet. And Tolstoy's Napoleon, in *War and Peace,* has always seemed much more lifelike than the Napoleon of the countless so-called biographies. They both have that reality which their literary creator gave them, a much less shaky reality than an historical portrait trying to be accurate.

You can of course find some features which the two categories of person do not share. The author never tells us everything about his characters. Nowhere in *Moby-Dick* are we told *which* of Captain Ahab's legs has been lost and replaced with a wooden one after his struggle with the white whale (an ambiguity, according to Umberto Eco, which John Huston was unable to respect when he had to take a decision about equipping Gregory Peck for the film). Since Melville didn't tell us, we shall never know. We can ask the same question about Byron – which was his club-foot? Apparently there are no clear indications (not that I have checked this out). But in the latter case, it is always possible to hope that one day someone will find the unpublished diary of a Venetian contessa who met him in Florian's, or crossing the Campo San Samuele, and noted this detail. And when I come to think of it, what about Talleyrand? When Sacha Guitry made his film *Le Diable boiteux*

(The lame devil), did he know which leg to limp with when he played the famous bishop-minister? Did he take the time to check, or was it a deliberately arbitrary choice, because in fact nobody knows?[3]

One extravagance is allowed to authors – and it adds a further dimension to their fictional nature: they can choose a pen name. When a literary character chooses a pseudonym, the author has to tell us about it so that we can appreciate it: for instance, when Jean Valjean in *Les Misérables* passes himself off as the honourable Monsieur Madeleine, or when in Balzac's *Père Goriot*, Jacques Collin registers at the Vauquer boarding house under the name of Vautrin. It would be pointless and completely irrelevant if Julien Sorel's real name (in Stendhal's *Scarlet and Black*) had *secretly* been Georges Bouton, or if Flaubert's Frédéric Moreau (in *Sentimental Education*) had been Auguste Lampin. The art of the novel is partly the art of omission, but some things can not be concealed from the reader.

It is hard to guess, unless you are a specialist, that Pierre Mac Orlan's real name was Pierre Dumarchey, Jean-Louis Curtis was Louis Laffitte, and that Anatole France's birth certificate says Anatole François Thibault. There may be good reason for publishing under a pseudonym – it may be out of discretion by people in certain senior posts (Saint-John Perse or Pierre-Jean Rémy), in order to reject their fathers (Stendhal), out of a wish to distinguish

3 Harold Bloom in the *New York Review of Books*, 24 September, 2009, writes that Byron was born "with a lame left foot". (J. B.)

between different books (Cécil Saint-Laurent/Jacques Laurent), or to simplify a foreign name (Henri Troyat started out as Lev Tarassov, Elsa Triolet as Elsa Kagan, and Teodor Józef Konrad Korzeniowski fortunately shortened his name to Joseph Conrad); from a desire to avoid a certain connotation (Marguerite de Crayencour chose to drop her aristocratic family name and become Marguerite Yourcenar); to disguise oneself during wartime (Jean Bruller took the name Vercors); or because one's original name had distracting connotations – so Georges Courteline dropped his name Georges Moinaux (which sounds like *moineau* = sparrow), and Philippe Sollers chose not to be the more precious Philippe Joyaux (which sounds like *joyau* = jewel); Gérard de Nerval went the other way, wanting to upgrade from his more ordinary name of Gérard Labrunie. Some cases might, however, require a more thorough psychological explanation: "Sébastien Japrisot", as a writer of crime novels, sounds fine, but what was wrong with his original name of Jean-Baptiste Rossi? And as for William Falkner altering the spelling to Faulkner, despite various scholarly explanations, I am still no wiser.

Authors and their characters do have something in common: they almost always have love lives. It is very rare for a novel to contain no love story at all. This subject is so huge and obvious that I will not go into it. But they also have sex lives. The narrative approach of an author to this subject will vary with style and temperament but also with the period of writing or the literary effect desired. It would no doubt be interesting, but not to our purpose here, to compare the ways novelists tackle physical sex. From Madame de Lafayette's *The Princesse de Clèves* to *L'histoire de dom B., portier des Chartreux* (The Story of Dom B., porter at the Charterhouse), ascribed to Jean-Charles Gervaise de Latouche, from complete silence to precise indeed anatomical detail, the variations are infinite. By the same token, one could look at the way people in novels eat – which might run from the briefest description ("They stopped at Mantes-la-Jolie where they consumed a light supper") to the most detailed: "He dipped a piece of rye bread into the sauce from the veal casserole whose aroma had pervaded the whole room, then, wiping his lips, tried the white Sancerre – it was a La Croix de Roy 1998, from the vineyards of Lucien Crochet – which the sommelier had served."

Authors do sometimes describe their own sex lives. This might be a literary exercise of complete sincerity (but is it really?); it might indicate a propensity to exhibitionism; and it might simply be a narrative procedure required by the text. I am quite certain, for example, that the famous book *My Secret Life*, which is supposed to be the exhaustive diary (in eleven volumes!) covering the sex life of a Victorian Englishman, is simply an erotic novel taking the form of a thoroughly explicit and total confession, in order to provoke the reader's interest. Yet Michel Foucault, in his preface to the French translation of extracts from it (*My Secret Life, Récit de la vie sexuelle d'un Anglais de l'époque victorienne*) presented the text as an authentic journal. And Jean-Jacques Pauvert, in his long preface to the full translation by Mathias Pauvert (*Ma vie secrète*), does not seem to doubt for a moment that this really was the auto-biographical account of one Henry Spencer Ashbee. Ashbee may indeed have been the author, but it is obvious to the reader that this is a novelistic narrative, a mixture of real-life experience and free-ranging fantasy.

Where sex life is concerned, the main difference between literary characters and authors is what I would call "sexual accounting" – not so much a matter of description but of numerical listing, usually in code, of a person's private sexual activity. It is of course so dry as to be virtually unreadable, and offers virtually no interest to the reader, so I do not think any author has taken the risk of depicting a character with this habit. One can indeed wonder what the point is (and that is the real mystery) even for the individual concerned to note down in a kind of technical way, without any sensual detail, what happened with whom, on what day. Perhaps since writers may have a heightened sense of the passage of time, of which sexuality is a critical symptom, the (male) writer may yield to the peculiar temptation of repeating these fleeting acts by committing them to the apparent eternity of writing.

My library contains at least two documents of this type: Benjamin Constant's *Journal* and Victor Hugo's *Carnets* (Note-books).

Benjamin Constant kept a journal during three periods of his life: from 6 January to 10 April, 1803; from early 1804 until the end of 1807; and from May 1811 to September 1816. What is relevant here is the "abbreviated journal" from 22 January, 1804 to 27

December, 1807. He explained this decision, which followed the death of his friend Madame Talma, the wife of the celebrated actor: "Madame Talma's death had thrown me into such deep depression that from that time, my journal, in which I had noted all the details of her illness, and sometimes passed a severe judgment on her character, became intolerable to me. But not wanting to abandon it completely, I decided to write it in a very abbreviated form, mostly in numbers".

The result for the reader – who was of course not supposed ever to see it – is rather astonishing: every day there are a few words and then some numbers from one to seventeen. For example the last few days of August 1804 are summed up as follows:

27: 4.2.2

28: 4.2

29: 4

30: 4.3

31: 4

That is an extreme example but not unique, so on 1 October, 1804 we read: 4.3.2.3. More often words and numbers appear side by side: 5 March, 1805: "Visit to Lacretelle. 4. Madame Dutertre 11. Letter from Minette 2.2." Or another example, 6 June, 1805: "Letter to Madame Dutertre, 2.12.4. but not much". This is of course completely meaningless to us – as it was meant to be – but I doubt whether even experts on military decoding or even computer analysts could manage to interpret the events which

Constant wanted to keep a note of, if it were not that he unintentionally helped us himself. Since he was afraid he might forget his own code, he wrote down the key to it at the end of the *Journal*. It goes like this:

1. signifies physical pleasure. 2. desire to break my eternal bond, so often considered. 3. return to this bond by memory or some momentary charm. 4. work. 5. discussion with my father. 6. feelings of affection for my father. 7. travel plans. 8. marriage plans. 9. fatigue. 10. touching memories and revival of love for Mme Lindsay. 11. hesitation over my intentions towards Mme Dutertre. 12. love for Mme Dutertre. 13. uncertainty about everything. 14. plan to settle in Dole to break with Biondetta. 15. plan to settle in Lausanne, for the same reason. 16. plans for overseas travel. 17. desire to be reconciled with certain enemies.

A rather disorienting list! It somewhat recalls Sei Shōnagon's list which contains among other headings: "Things that cause distress / Things that one has neglected the end of / Things that make one's heart beat faster / Things that annoy one / Things recalling a sweet memory from the past / Things that are painful / Things that fill you with anguish / Things that appear upsetting / Things that are incompatible / Things that are distasteful to see / Things that distract you when you are bored" and so on (*The Pillow Book*). In Constant's case, all sorts of things are mixed up: emotions and plans, factual details and complex states of mind, simple elements and others which are more involved: "the desire to be reconciled with certain enemies"! But it does give some idea of the confusion of his feelings – see, for example, the entry for 30 September, 1804: "Dined at Bosset. 3.2.3" and other days full of different emotions: "Write to Mme de Staël. 2.8.7.12.4. Went well. Spent the day alone. 1".

More details would be informative not only about Benjamin Constant but about the human condition more generally. To be honest, number 1 is not the one that crops up most often, certainly less than 4, but it does appear fairly regularly, either without any context (so how did Constant know what he meant, if he read it a few years later?) or with some annotation suggesting a regular practice. So in 1804, on 26 May, 22 June, 28 June, 30 June, 3 July, 18 July, the famous 1 is preceded by "Went to Geneva", which of course tells us nothing, but must have reminded him of the circumstances. Fortunately he took this secret to the grave.

Victor Hugo, in this domain as in so many others, had more baroque practices. He didn't keep a journal but wrote entries in his private notebooks, which were a form of domestic and sexual accounting. The two were sometimes combined, since he sometimes paid the "ladies" who provided him with certain services: prostitutes during his stay in Brussels, servants or infrequent visitors in Jersey, or the actresses, would-be actresses and women in need who flocked round him when he made his glorious re-entry to Paris after the fall of the Second Empire. I don't intend to go into either his love life or his sex life – they fairly quickly became separate compartments in his case. But his meticulous accounts covered several decades. Like Benjamin Constant, he used code or foreign languages, chiefly to evade the jealous curiosity of his lover, Juliette Drouet. A few examples among thousands of these jumbled notes, with decoding assistance from Henri Guillemin, *Hugo et la sexualité* (Hugo's sexuality):

27 January: Charlotte *cloche* [= bell, an allusion to ringing the bell in Scene One of his play *L'Epée* (The sword)].

28 April: Mlle C. Rosiers, *piernas* [= legs]

3 May: B.C.R. [= *Baisé* Catherine Rosiers = sex with Catherine Rosiers]

22 July: 3 francs [French equivalent of] f.w.f.m.i.b.n. (for waiting for me in bedroom, naked)

13 March: Catherine. *sub clara nuda lucerna* [naked under lamplight]

[undated]: Emile [for Emilie] Taffart, rue du cirque, 21, 6e, osc [osculum = kiss, in Latin] 4 fr 50

8 September: Marie. Saints [= *seins* = breasts]

10 September: *Misma. Pecho. Todo.* [Same, breast, everything]

17 February: Marietta: Garter [in English in the original]

20 February: Mme Robert [Zélia] b.d.b. [= *besa de boca* = kiss on the lips]

24 November: E. G. *Esta manana. Todo* [Elisa Grapillot. This morning. Everything]

As well as this mish-mash of abbreviations, borrowings from Spanish, English and Latin, and puns, Victor Hugo also played word games with women's names, no doubt amusing himself: *Esther*hazy (Esther); Natte-à-lit (Nathalie); Eb*louisse*ment = "dazzling", contains the name Louise; Alphonse Inn (= Alphonsine); "*Anna*les de Schaerbeck" (Anna); "Question deli*cate: rhinoceros*" (Catherine) and so on. And a certain number of cabbalistic signs (crosses, wavy lines, circles, underlinings and dashes, a sort of capital T on its side) probably meant something too, but they are still awaiting the literary equivalent of the deciphering of the Rosetta Stone.

I don't mean to belittle Hugo by referring to this sort of accounting, just to express my astonishment at how important it evidently was to him. As Guillemin tells us, Victor Hugo expressly ordered all his manuscripts to be deposited in the French National Library, "even fragments of poetry or a single line; any text which is written in my hand". In other words, so that we, his posterity, can find them and read them: "When I am no longer there, people will see what I was like" – a strange sentence.

Stendhal, in spite of appearances, does not really go in for this kind of book-keeping. True, in his journal he does refer, among many other things, to his love affairs and sexual adventures, and does occasionally use English or Italian to do so. But it is a more literary kind of reference. So of his affair with Angela Pietragrua, he wrote on 21 September, 1811, "Yesterday, I received a half-favour", and a little later, "On 21 September *at* [in English] 11.30,

I won this victory so long desired". But he cannot refrain from immediately reflecting on the event. "Nothing is missing from my happiness, except what would be happiness for an idiot – that it is not a victory. It seems to me that perfectly pure pleasure can only be the result of intimacy. The first time [in English] it is a victory; 'in the three *suivantes*' [in franglais = the next three times] one attains intimacy. Then comes perfect happiness, if she is a woman of intelligence, and character, whom one loves." Two years later, in Monza, he wrote, "I see from my braces that it was on 21 September at 11.30 in the morning". Stendhal's book-keeping is much more feeling than a simple sexual tally, and a man who writes on his braces the date and hour of his amorous "victory" can't be all bad.

Victor Hugo was sure enough of himself to be able to leave behind a record of his less attractive features. Henri Beyle (a.k.a. Stendhal), who adopted over a hundred pseudonyms in his life, writes somewhere in *Memoirs of an Egotist*: "I found I had every possible fault; I would have preferred to be someone else". How are we to distinguish between the real and the fictional in his "Henry Brulard", who is presented to us by the author as his double – but which one?

8

THE WORLD WITHIN REACH

Like all the men in the Library, I travelled in my youth:
I went on pilgrimages looking for a single book,
or perhaps for the catalogue of catalogues.

JORGE LUIS BORGES

One episode of *The Twilight Zone*, the famous American sci-fi television serial of the 1960s, broadcast in France as *La Quatrième Dimension* (The fourth dimension), tells the story of a bank clerk who can never find time to indulge in his favourite activity: reading. At home, his wife makes a scene if he picks up a book, and at work, reading behind the counter would get him into trouble. One day, after he has taken refuge in the strongroom with a book, there is a huge explosion – an atom bomb presumably – which destroys his town, leaving him the sole survivor. After hours of despair, he recovers the will to live when he finds that the local library has remained intact. He enthusiastically draws up a programme of books to read in the coming days, weeks and months, and just when everything seems to be going well, he drops his spectacles on the floor, where their thick lenses shatter into fragments. The episode was called "Time enough at last" and one could read it as a metaphor for bibliomania: the man who fights melancholy and depression through reading, who reaches a point when he has as many books as he wants – and then drops dead.

The library protects us from external enemies, filters the noise of the world, tempers the cold winds around us – but also gives us the feeling of being all-powerful. For the library makes our puny human capabilities fade into insignificance: it concentrates time and space. It contains on its shelves all the strata of the past. The centuries that have gone before us are there. ("[Writing is] great, very great, in enabling us to converse with the dead, the absent, and the unborn, at all distances of time and space" – Abraham Lincoln.) The past haunts libraries, not only in documents bearing witness to past ages, but through scholarly works, literary reconstructions and images of all kinds. But my library is also a concentrate of space. Every region on earth is represented there somewhere, the continents with all their landscapes, their climates and their ways of life. Even imaginary countries like Swift's Lilliput, Musil's Cacania, Buzatti's Desert of the Tartars, Faulkner's Yoknapatawpha County. Or places little known to humans but explored by authors – Ray Bradbury's *Martian Chronicles*, Dante's *Inferno,* or Cyrano de Bergerac's *Voyages to the Moon and the Sun.* I can be transported there in an instant, change my mind immediately, or even find myself in two places at once. All this has something divine about it – which is perhaps why when we talk about libraries, we so easily think in religious terms. Borges parodied Nicholas of Cusa: "The library is a sphere, of which the true centre is some kind of hexagon, and the surface of which is inaccessible". Umberto Eco uttered this strange pronouncement: "If God existed, he would be a library". And surely that must refer to the way it enables us to overcome time and space.

And here – since my intention is not to write about the authors who matter most deeply to me – I will not be talking about what it means to be living in daily contact with them. ("With few books, but learned ones / I live in conversation with the dead / And I listen to the deceased with my eyes" – Francisco de Quevedo.) For beyond books themselves, there is everything they have to tell us about the human condition. Pointing out that the past allows us to put our own present into salutary perspective is something of a truism, yet surprisingly many people seem not to know it. To cite just one example, which touches me nearly, if you delve into history, you see how individuals come into and out of focus as fashions change: J. S. Bach was forgotten for a century until he was rediscovered thanks to Mendelssohn; Shakespeare was unknown in France until Voltaire and above all the romantics; Georges de la Tour had vanished from memory for two hundred years – and the same was even true of Vermeer! Jean Cocteau relates in his *Journal* that when Jean-Pierre Melville's film *Les Enfants terribles* came out in 1950, the soundtrack contained a keyboard piece by Vivaldi, but he could not find a single recording of *The Four Seasons* in any Paris record shop. To take some recent examples, it is easy nowadays to express a liking for Impressionism, Cubism or abstract painting, since our age has assimilated what was once new and shocking. But who is to say whether in 1880 I would have preferred Manet and Renoir to Bouguereau and Cabanel? More seriously, would I have been a pro-Dreyfusard when it really mattered, or opposed to the Munich agreement in time to make a difference? People more intelligent than I came down on the wrong side. Lucien Febvre writes somewhere that anachronism is the mortal sin of historians, but it is also a common failing among ordinary people, and one has to be aware of it and try to fight it.

But to return to the library. Once it has been established, it tends to become an unavoidable transit zone for reality, a sort of vortex that sucks in everything that happens to us. That catalogue you want to find a place for on the shelf becomes an integral part of the visit to the exhibition or museum, as does the documentation about a town and its monuments discovered in the depths of Portugal, Italy or France. What bliss it is, after a day in a city you have always meant to visit, as you sit in your hotel room at the end of the afternoon, looking through the books, postcards and brochures destined to find their way to your bookshelves, all giving you the comforting feeling that you are taking home some tangible elements of what has already become the past! It gives you the impression of safeguarding some fragments of lost time, whereas everything else, the emotions and sensation of the journey, will be fleeting memories.

Michel Melot points out in *La bibliothèque multimédia contemporaine* (The contemporary multimedia library) that "The library has always been connected to a set of practices for acquiring knowledge, not only to the book. In Alexandria it was part of a greater whole, the Museum." Yes, libraries do accept other things: periodicals, engravings, posters, pamphlets and so on. Melot was talking about public libraries, of course, but things are much the same in private libraries, allowing for the different scale of resources (an individual can't have a copyright library!) and for the more limited obligations (I don't have to be at anyone's service but my own). So I don't keep many newspapers, for instance, but I do keep a lot of cuttings. Articles have two possible destinations, either being placed inside a book where they have their logical place, and will therefore be easy to remember, or in a big box of "articles to keep", in which, as a rule, I can never find what I'm looking for. I have even gone so far as to buy a book, because it had a connection with an article I wanted to slip inside it and be sure of finding again, if need be.

As well as all this, I have music and film sections, like a modern multi-media library. The desire to have anything that is really worthwhile within arm's reach is not confined to books. It is in any case hard to separate cinema and literature, music and reading. C.D.s and D.V.D.s have the advantage of taking up less room than books and above all it is easy to shelve them because they have a standard format. Films are a problem though: where will I ever find the time to see the ones which – in spite of all my self-denying ordinances – find their way into my home? Luckily, they are very easy to classify (alphabetical order of title, with occasional boxed sets by director integrated into the order, and a few rare exceptions, such as boxed sets on themes). My C.D.s are arranged by genre, and then by alphabetical order of composer or performer, the difficulty there being that some discs are a mixture – a performer playing works by several composers – and I sometimes hesitate over the category of music. Where do I put traditional or folk music? Should gospel and blues go in with jazz? Should I keep classical and contemporary music separate? And I see that a sort of bookish deformation has absurdly pushed me to put tango, flamenco and salsa all in one place, and fado and bossa nova somewhere else. And then there is the occasional nasty surprise when the sleeve is empty or fails to contain the right disc.

But the library is governed by a wider economy, to do with one's relation to the outside world. To play its part properly, the library must be left behind from time to time, so that one can miss it and then gratefully rediscover it. From a distance, it becomes idealized, and helps one to bear the discomfort of travelling. It is waiting for us at home and is already being enriched with the things we are bringing back with us.

Like public libraries, my bookshelves hold a number of reference works. Putting it briefly, these are mainly books that help me to use other books: dictionaries of my own language, of foreign languages, dictionaries of literature, history, religion, philosophy, psychoanalysis, sociology, mathematics, physics, astronomy, and so on. Some of them I consult every day, but most of them have been opened only once, the day I bought them. Their presence is reassuring however – and you never know! Two years ago, I suddenly needed, while doing a tricky translation, to look up something in the Compact Edition of the *Oxford English Dictionary*, the one that comes with a magnifying glass on account of the very small print – and although it is described as "compact", it has taken up a lot of room for the last thirty years. It is true that the *Essai de grammaire slovène* (Essay on Slovenian grammar) by Claude Vicenot is unlikely ever to be of the slightest use to me. But this is a souvenir from several visits to Ljubljana, and I would feel I was blotting out my past if I got rid of it. (I still have a photo, taken with Nicole Zand, in Lipiza in 1987 or 1988, by Eugen Bavcar, a Slovenian photographer – who is blind.) Another unusual scene remains in my mind from this trip: with a group of writers of various nationalities, we were at Gorizia, at an agricultural show, and in a vast marquee where beer and slivovitz were flowing freely. Carried away by the atmosphere, the Hungarian writer Peter Esterházy and the Yugoslav Danilo Kiš – who died shortly afterwards of throat cancer – got up and started waltzing together among the tables crowded with local peasants raising their glasses. And I see that next to it in the shelf is a French-Corsican dictionary (compiled by "I Culioli": Jean Dominique, Antoine Louis, Gabriel Xavier and Vannina Sandra), which I had completely forgotten about, but once I opened it I found it hard to put down. So, for instance, I came across the French word "gluant" (= sticky) for which the Corsican is "adj.: *lumacosu, vischjosu, mustosu, appiccicarinu* (of a person who clings on to one)". Without really understanding the etymology, I love the fascinating thought of being able to describe someone who will not let me go as "*appicci-carinu*": the meaning of the word seems to go perfectly with its pronunciation.

So anyway, on the shelves behind my desk there are plenty of standard dictionaries, but also a few which are somewhat extravagant. Their titles are not without a certain fantastical poetry: the *Dictionnaire des onomatopées* (Onomatopoeic dictionary) by Pierre Enckell and Pierre Rézeau; the *Dictionnaire des langues imaginaires* (Dictionary of imaginary languages) by Paolo Albani and Berlinghiero Buonarroti; *Les Sept Merveilles – les expressions chiffrées, jamais deux sans trois, les neuf muses, faire la une* (The seven wonders, expressions of number: never two without three, the nine muses, to make the front page – "page one" in French) by Jean-Claude Bologne;[4] *Les Fous littéraires* (Literary Madmen) by André Blavier; *Le Dictionnaire du monde rural* (Dictionary of the rural world) by Marcel Lachiver; *Le Rose* by Annie Mollard-Desfour (part of the sequence of dictionaries of words and expressions using colours published by CNRS Editions); *L'Etonnante Histoire des noms des mammifères* (The amazing story of the names of mammals) by Henriette Walter and Pierre Avenas; the more prosaic *Dictionnaire du français régional du Berry-Bourbonnais* (Dictionary of French spoken in the Berry-Bourbonnais regions) by Pierrette Dubuisson and Marcel Bonnin; not forgetting the *Dictionnaire des saints imagi-*

4 Now under another title: *Une de perdue, dix de retrouvées: chiffres et nombres dans les expressions de la langue francaise,* 2004.

naires et facétieux (Dictionary of imaginary and facetious Saints) by Jacques E. Merceron. And I have the very recent *Dictionnaire de la pluie* (Dictionary of rain), by Patrick Boman. A dictionary is not just a useful instrument: it can often be an original way of approaching a subject, casting light on it in a special way. The *Dictionnaire Hitchcock* (ed. Laurent Bourdon, Larousse, 2007) is quite distinct from all the monographs on Alfred Hitchcock, as well as from Donald Spoto's biography. And the *Dictionnaire Marcel Proust*, edited by Annick Bouillaguet and Brian G. Rogers (Honoré Champion, 2004), was a useful addition to a bibliography which is admittedly already vast. In any case, since all dictionaries are by definition incomplete or contain errors, one tends to accumulate them in order to compare one with another. I have several dictionaries from the nineteenth century in my library: Vapereau's *Dictionnaire des littératures*, Bouillet's *Dictionnaire d'histoire et de géographie*; Dezobry and Bachelet's *Dictionnaire de biographie, d'histoire, de géographie, des antiquités et des institutions*, but not the *Grand Larousse*. Since our idea of fame or notoriety has changed, one can find in these works names of people or subjects which have disappeared from more recent dictionaries, and they are also notable for a more personal and idiosyncratic tone. I have a second edition of the *Dictionnaire de la conversation et de la lecture* (Dictionary of conversation and reading) which describes itself as follows: "A reasoned inventory of the most indispensable notions for all, by an association of scholars and men of letters under the editorship of M. W. Duckett, second edition entirely revised, corrected and augmented by thousands of the most up-to-date entries. Librairie de Firmin Didot Frères, Fils et Cie, Printers to the Institut de France, rue Jacob, 56. MDCCCLXXIII." It is indeed a dictionary, as it says, but instead of contenting itself with brief definitions, it does not hesitate to plunge into long perorations. Guided by the magic of alphabetical chance, we find five entries starting on page 136 of the first volume as follows: *Adule* (marbles of): Adule (Adulis), ancient port then in Ethiopia, now in Eritrea (followed by about fifteen lines); then *Adulte* (Adult) about twenty lines; *Adultération* gets only four lines but *Adultère* (Adultery) gets four entire columns, while *Adustion* which comes next is dispatched in two lines ("a term in surgery: cauterizing or burning"). My series is, alas, incomplete, and ends at Volume XV with *Saxons / Saxonnes* (m. and f. "Germanic peoples"). What a pity – it irresistibly brings to mind a character in Jules Renard's *L'Ecornifleur* (The scrounger) who, in exchange for a dinner to which he invites himself every night, provides interesting conversation. It gradually dawns on you as the story goes on that the subjects he introduces to the conversation, day after day, are in alphabetical order. (I have just found a recent edition of Renard's little novel and, on reading it, am flabbergasted to find that, no, there is no trace of the alphabetical nature of the "hero's" culture! Did I confuse this one with some other literary figure who did the same, or did the adapter of the television version, which I saw in the days of black and white, take liberties with the original text? Jacques Duby played the scrounger. Did the film and the novel get mixed up in my memory? Who knows?)

You might think that the internet has changed all that. Yes, of course, it has. And that is one of the reasons that drove me to write this little book. Would I ever have put together the same library if I had been born into the internet generation? Almost certainly not. If we are to believe the statistical surveys of the time spent on average in front of a computer or television screen, when does anyone find time to read? The internet and the many television channels have driven out the boredom which was always the prime motive for reading, but should we regret it? What is more, we now have the convenience of being able to order books online (new or second-hand); and the availability of basic texts, along with the digitizing of others, has made it far easier to locate a particular passage. These novelties have unavoidably transformed the status of the library: it is only one among many ways of acquiring knowledge. And they have changed the status of the book, which is just one method among others, and not the most accessible, of finding "entertainment". But the art book, for example, will not be much affected by the phenomenon. Even if there are more and more images on the internet, they aren't always the ones you want, and the screen is not really adapted to consulting text and image at the same time. As for reading *War and Peace* or leafing through numbers of *L'Os à Moelle* (The marrow bone) edited by Pierre Dac (Omnibus edition, 2007), the hard copy version, as they say, probably still has a future.

The problem in years to come will not be how to accumulate books in order to have them within reach, but to find one's way through the exponentially growing mass of publications. In France alone there were 60,000 new titles published in 2006, compared with 30,000 twenty years ago; and, worldwide, a million titles in 2000, compared with 250,000 in 1950. This is bound to change the way booksellers work. They are unable to carry everything in store, so will increasingly have to select and filter. Large booksellers with online ordering, which are less willing to vet their titles carefully, or to make more cultural investment in their commercial practice, will remain efficient multipliers of the success initiated by others. But even their commercial margins may suffer if they are obliged – as part of France's law on the single retail book price insists – to make their customers pay the price of postage and packing, as one of these booksellers recently told me, and as certain recent decisions in the courts seem to suggest. (This precedent has recently been challenged in the appeal court.)

In fact, for my generation, the internet is a valuable extra, but it is only an extra. For example, a few months ago, I had to identify about a thousand French film titles relating to "noir" films, mostly American in origin, referred to in an Italian book. Without the existence of several Italian film-buff websites, I would never have managed it. And I found up-to-date information there which none of the books on my shelves could manage – obviously, since they could only cover the period up to three or four years ago. What is more, I have benefited from a classic book-based education, which means I have a particular view of the internet. What will be the approach of the generations who are growing up with it? Who knows whether it will be better or worse, but it will certainly be different. I am not very good at using search engines, but they fit into a specific, pre-established scheme in my head. It's the same for figures: I learnt mathematics in the days of multiplication tables and mental arithmetic, so I don't need a calculator, but on the other hand, my mental calculations are certainly slower than a machine. As Robert Musil put it, "All progress forward is at the same time a step backward." History shows that you never escape unscathed from a beneficial form of progress.

Oddly enough, the infinite source of information which the internet provides does not have for me the same magical status as my library. Here I am in front of my computer, I can look up anything I want, jumping even further in time and space than through my books, but there's something missing: that touch of the divine. Perhaps it's something physical: I'm only using my fingertips: the whole process is outside me, going through a screen and a machine. Nothing like these walls lined with books which I know – almost – by heart. On one hand, I feel as if have a fabulous artificial arm, able to move about in that interstellar space outside, while on the other, I am inside a womb whose walls are my book-lined shelves – the archetype in literature would be the inside of the *Nautilus*, 20,000 leagues under the sea. As you see, it is not always a rational matter.

9
PHANTOMS IN THE LIBRARY

fantôme: [phantom] A sheet or card inserted
to mark the place of a book removed from a library shelf,
or a document which has been borrowed.

PETIT LAROUSSE

Yes, libraries too can die. Great, official public libraries are
sometimes spectacularly assassinated – burnt down or bombed,
like the libraries of Alexandria, the Louvre library after the Paris
Commune of 1871 (not to mention the libraries of the Conseil
d'Etat and the Hôtel de Ville), the library of Holland House in
London in 1940 – the scene of the famous photograph – the library
in Dresden in 1945, the library in Sarajevo in 1992, and so many
others. Bombed, burnt out, and often witnessing their contents
finished off by the efforts of firemen to save them. There is a mar-
tyrology of libraries by Lucien X. Polastron, *Livres en feu, histoire de
la destruction sans fin des bibliothèques* (*Books on Fire: the destruction of
libraries*): this is one of the books I have found most painful
to read in all my days as a reader, tragically justifying its sub-title.
Public libraries may also be dispersed, going by some of the
books I have bought second-hand which still retain traces of their
origins. Just on a bookcase within reach, I find the French edition

of Anthony Blunt's *Artistic Theory in Italy* (Julliard, 1962), which still has its shelf mark (701.17/B659T) and a label from the library of the Saint-Augustin Cap Rouge Seminary in Quebec. No doubt its presence on my shelves indicates a falling-off in the number of vocations. As for Millard Meiss's *The Painter's Choice*, this comes from the South Regional Library of Miami-Dade county. Has the library disappeared, was the book stolen, or was it a victim of what is sometimes known as "weeding" or "pruning" – in other words, throwing out books that are too seldom borrowed? Laurence Santantonios informs us that in a former underground car park in the eleventh *arrondissement* of Paris there are five kilometres of shelves holding some of the books weeded from the city's sixty local municipal libraries: the rest have been pulped or distributed to charities, prisons or hospitals. In this strange location, there are apparently 180,000 books available for potential borrowers. Perhaps American libraries have more radical policies? At any rate, somehow some of these books have found their way to me.

As for the risks faced by private libraries, Nodier quotes his friend Peignot: "The three enemies of the book are rats, worms and dust, to which we must add a fourth: borrowers." Rats, or rather mice, seem from my own observations to prefer newsprint, and are happy in my case to attack the hundreds of copies of the *New York Review of Books* or *Times Literary Supplement* which I have kept religiously, without ever consulting them (because how would I manage to retrieve something from wobbly piles five feet high?). I seem so far to have been spared by worms, unless it is just that

I have not yet discovered their ravages. Dust, yes, there's plenty of that, but you can always dust off a book when you need to consult it. The idea of keeping my books behind glass I find, for some inexplicable reason, quite impossible. As for the saying "a book lent is a book lost", the solution is very simple: never lend a book, always give it away. Then things are absolutely clear. It has to be applied within limits of course! And there is the delicate matter of divorce, becoming more frequent in society nowadays, and the risk it poses to the survival of libraries which were once shared between spouses. But the psycho-sociological complexity of this question would take us too far. The reasonable solution, but perhaps difficult to put into practice, would be to have separate libraries. Short of that, common sense or prudence might dictate that when people put their two book collections together, they hang on to duplicate copies and keep a discreet record of who bought what.

Private libraries do sometimes burn down too. I know personally of three examples. In the first case, the owner's flat in the rue Bonaparte in Paris burnt down when he was on a sailing trip. When he got back, all he had left was a pair of shorts, his swimming trunks, espadrilles and a few T-shirts. In the second, the owners, two writers and teachers, divorced shortly afterwards – was there a connection? The third case was that of my friend Pierre B., just a few weeks ago. It happened while he was asleep, so he might never have woken in time. And in such cases everything goes – photographs, pictures, family mementoes, letters and other possessions. To lose one's books is to lose one's past. In Pierre B.'s case, all I could offer him by way of consolation for the moment were two quotations I had found while writing this book. One is by Valincour, Racine's successor in the Académie Française, who, after losing his books in a fire, declared: "I would have derived little benefit from my books if I had not learnt to do without them". The other is from Manguel: "During dinner, Anders Björsson confided to me that when a fire completely destroyed his library, he suddenly realized that before he tried to reconstitute it, he would have to know which books *not* to include" – *A Reading Diary*. Apart from accidental fires, one has to reckon with the occasional *auto-da-fé* or ceremonial book-burning. One of the earliest was decreed in 213 B.C.E. by the first ruler of the Middle Kingdom, Qin Shi Huangdi (the builder of the Great Wall), on the advice of his minister Li Si. Orders went out for the immediate destruction of all books which were not on medicine, agriculture or divination. The chronicles tell us that a certain number of learned men preferred to die rather than destroy their libraries. Violent and systematic destruction of books has occurred time out of mind in history, and has almost always accompanied or preceded the persecution of their potential readers. We have only to recall the book-burning ordered by Goebbels on 10 May, 1933, on the Opernplatz in Berlin, followed by about thirty other similar events throughout Germany. Or the university library in Algiers, which was blown up by the extreme settler organization, the O.A.S., on 6 June, 1962, two months after the referendum approving the Evian Agreements on Algerian independence. ("Burning a book, or writing one, are the two actions between which culture's contrary pendulum swings are plotted" – Maurice Blanchot.)

The only advantage of a library like mine is that it has never interested the few burglars who have honoured me with a visit: the books are too heavy and would have little resale value. As second-hand dealers often say, "I don't take books any more, I've got nowhere to keep them and they don't sell." But then there is the case of José Mindlin, a Brazilian bibliophile who was held up about ten years ago in his house, which was also his library. The gangsters took his wife hostage, and gave him an afternoon to find the ransom money. Before he set off to do the round of the banks, they said that if he failed to come back with the money, they would not harm his wife but would set fire to his library. He paid up. Mindlin also tells the tale of how he once flew to Paris to buy a book he had been pursuing for seventeen years – *O Guarani* by José de Alencar (The Guarani), 1857, and then left it on the plane taking him back to Brazil. "Luckily," he adds, "Air France found it for me."

A bibliomaniac may decide to sell his library. Galantaris quotes the example of two collectors who could not help trying to buy back their own books at the auction they had themselves organized: the Comte de la Bédoyère and Baron Jérôme Pichon. The latter spent the remaining seventeen years of his life buying back those of his books which, despite his best efforts, had been dispersed that day. ("If a man wants to taste in a single moment the bitterest misery here on earth, let him sell his books" – Jules Janin.)

But in any case, private libraries – except for one or two which have been preserved intact, such as those of Charles Spoelberch de Lovenjoul (a Belgian collector who left his books to the Institut de France), Jacques Doucet in Paris, or Martin Bodmer in Geneva – usually disappear when their "curator" dies. Inheritors don't know what to do with a mass of books that is of no interest to them and which takes up such a lot of room. They may even have some pecuniary interest in their haste to sell, but perhaps too they are taking revenge on the books that posed such a visible problem in their own past. I remember once, on a wintry Saturday morning on the Place des Prêcheurs in Aix-en-Provence, seeing hundreds of books belonging to the late Monsieur G., dean of the faculty, being sold off. A whole scholarly career was laid out there, open to the sky, on casual and, as it were, surreptitious sale to anyone passing by. A few of us looked through books dedicated to him: "To Dean G. with my warmest admiration"; "To Dean G, in gratitude for . . . " and so on, and leafed through the entire run of the *Revue balzacienne*, the academic journal at the heart of his research (he was a Balzac specialist). Thus ended a life of study and erudition. He had built up the Faculty of Letters in Aix to be the leading centre it became in the 1960s and '70s. I bought a few modest volumes, as a posthumous homage to a man whom, as it happens, I had never met. Another example is the way that Georges Dumézil's library was dispersed after his death. There was an element of settling scores about that. The only section that was saved, I believe, thanks to Georges Charachidzé, his long-time collaborator, was his collection of books on the Caucasus. That reminds me

irresistibly of Catherine de Medici, who, the day after the accidental death of her husband Henri II, confiscated the crown jewels he
had given to his mistress, Diane de Poitiers, and obliged her to
vacate Chenonceaux and move to the less spectacular chateau of
Chaumont-sur-Loire. Lucien Polastron tells the story of Prince
Mahmud al-Dawla ibn Fatik who in the Middle Ages had the
largest library in Cairo:

> The prince loved nothing so much as reading and writing
> and he would devote himself to his passion every evening,
> on dismounting from his horse. He was a talented poet.
> When he died suddenly, his wife, also a princess from
> the reigning dynasty, ordered his slaves to collect all
> Mahmud's books in the courtyard inside the palace. And
> there she chanted a funeral dirge, as she slowly threw into
> the great fountain, one after another, all the books which
> had deprived her of his love.

There are other phantoms too. Diderot had the double good
fortune to live to see Catherine the Great of Russia buying his
entire library, while allowing him the run of it, and also receiving
1000 livres a year for "the trouble and care he will give to shape this
library". And still in Russia, Varlam Shalamov, who spent much of
his life in Stalin's labour camps, starts his little book of which the
French title is *Mes Bibliothèques* (My libraries): "At three years old,
the earliest I can remember, I owned the first and last library I

have ever had: it consisted of two books *Ah-ee, Du-du!* and Tolstoy's *Alphabet.*" He ends the book, which is in fact an account of the rare and precious occasions when he was able to read during his twenty or so years in the Gulag, with a sentence as simple as it is heavy with sadness: "To my regret, I have never owned a library of my own."

There are some accidental librarians – they succeeded where Pessoa failed. Marcel Duchamp was employed at the Bibliothèque Sainte-Geneviève in Paris for the two years before his departure for the United States in 1915, and for four years in the early 1920s, André Breton was a part-time librarian – at a salary of 500 francs a month – for Jacques Doucet. And I cannot resist the anecdote, also in the twentieth century, of Henri Matisse, who, having run out of money in 1903, applied for the post of "controller of the law on the poor" because he was intrigued by the job title. It would have brought him 1200 francs a year if he had been successful – but only three of the one hundred candidates were chosen; and despite having a number of people put in a word for him, he was not one of them. Thus does our destiny hang by a thread – one of the great artists of the twentieth century might have become a Sunday painter.

In June 1784, at a dinner given by Sebastiano Foscarini, Venetian ambassador to Vienna, Giacomo Casanova made the acquaintance of Count Joseph Charles Waldstein, the emperor's chamberlain. Won over by the brilliant conversation of the adventurer, who was like himself a freemason, Waldstein proposed that he take the post of librarian of the 40,000 volumes in his castle at Dux in Bohemia (today Duchkov in the Czech Republic). Casanova, who had just been taken on by Foscarini to "write dispatches", and who was – as usual – deep in amorous intrigues, did not take up the offer. But, the following year the ambassador died and Casanova, having failed to find suitable employment, went to Töplitz, as others might to Canossa, to meet the chamberlain, who offered him the job again, at a salary of 1000 florins a year (about 30,000 Euros in today's money). In the event, Casanova did not find it easy to live in the lugubrious castle, so far from his past exploits. Despite various attempts to flee, he ended up spending the last thirteen years of his life there. Was he disagreeable to the rest of the staff, as the Prince of Ligne, Waldstein's uncle suggests? "Not a day went past when there wasn't some uproar in the household over his coffee, or his milk, or the dish of macaroni he insisted on." Or did he just become a scapegoat for his fellow employees? Both, probably. Casanova in decline must have been odious, and the count's household staff were no doubt on the rustic side. It was boredom that drove him to write his *Story of My Life*; boredom and the hope of escape in imagination from loneliness and old age, to relive through the pen the amorous adventures, now no longer possible in reality. ("My memories are more exciting than the life I am leading now, madam", he wrote to a correspondent.) Casanova does not appear to have made much use of the castle library, which would have enabled him to ornament his preface with impressive quotations from such as Cicero, Petrarch, Virgil, Horace, Pliny, Martial or Cornelius Nepos. A life made up of dalliance, worldly pleasures and trivialities was in those days no obstacle to showing off one's learning – on the contrary. He died at Dux on 4 June, 1798, and was buried in St Barbara's churchyard. A few years earlier, Lessing, the author of *Laokoon*, had been obliged, in order to survive, to take a post as librarian for the Duke of Brunswick at Wolfenbüttel. His eight-year stay there was extremely troubled. He lost his wife in childbirth and the baby died too; but here it was that he also wrote his most famous play, *Emilia Galotti*.

Another sad fate was that of Herman Melville. In 1853, after the failure of his novel *Pierre*, he tried to find a consular posting (Honolulu, Florence, Antwerp, Glasgow). To no avail. Not even with the support of his father-in-law, Judge Shaw, of Richard Dana, author of the successful book *Two Years Before the Mast*, of his uncle Pierre Gansevoort, and of Nathaniel Hawthorne, who had himself been appointed American consul in Liverpool the year before. To cap it all, a fire at his publishers, Harper's, destroyed the plates of his books and virtually all the copies they had in stock. He tried again for the Florence post in 1860 and once more had political backing. He was received at the White House by Lincoln, who had just been elected, but he failed that time too. "A job, who will give me a job?" Not until 1866 did he manage to get the humblest of "grace and favour" posts as a customs inspector. For twenty years or so, he paced the quaysides in New York and watched pulling in and out of harbour the ships on which he had begun his sailing and writing career. One might mention his strange relationship with Hawthorne, fifteen years his elder, to whom he dedicated *Moby-Dick* and whom he visited in Liverpool in 1856, both on the way to the Holy Land and on the way back. One might go on to wonder at the unusual work, *Hawthorne*, published by Henry James in 1879, fifteen years after Hawthorne's death, in the series *English Men of Letters*. This is ostensibly a homage, but on closer inspection it turns out to be a subtle and smiling execution of the writer who had imprudently preceded the first truly European American author: Henry James himself.

To return to Portugal, in the month of November 1983, where I began this book, I had gone to Cintra on the track of the love affair between Carlos Eduardo da Maia and Maria Eduarda, the tragic lovers created by Eça de Queiros. And in Coimbra, I decided not to make use of a telephone number, which I had in my pocket: it was that of Miguel Torga, whose books *Arche* and *En franchise intérieure, pages de journal 1933–1977* (Intimate frankness, pages from my journal) I had just read with pleasure. People had told me that he was very approachable and spoke French (his wife was Belgian) but I felt too strongly the fear of creating an artificial situation by bothering someone because one admires his books, and of the inevitable conversation that would follow. So I did nothing about it. I still don't regret it. In Buçaco, up above Coimbra, I had a strange "Valery Larbaud" moment. And when I got back to France I realized that the text I had irresistibly been reminded of there, *200 chambres, 200 salles de bains* (200 bedrooms, 200 bathrooms), which Valery Larbaud had dedicated to Jean Paulhan in 1926, had indeed been written in this former hunting-lodge of the kings of Portugal, nowadays the Palace Hotel, remarkably placed as it is in the middle of a forest fragrant with rare essences.

I still have a little dictionary of conversational Portuguese, which I found in a second-hand shop in the Baixa district of Lisbon. This *Guia da conversaçao Portuguez-Francez para uso dos viantes et dos estudiantes* (Portuguese-French conversational guide for travellers and students) by J. I. Roquette, was published, the imprint tells us, by "Ch. Fouraut & son, having acquired the international bookshop of Ch. Hingray, 47 rue Saint-André des Arts in Paris", though *when* I don't know, since it carries no publication date. But it must have been before 1888, when a certain Mlle Julietta de Campos Vidal wrote her name all over the title page. This is a handy-size little book containing a vocabulary (beginning as is only proper with God, the Creator and Christ: *Deos / Dieu, O Creador / Le Créateur / O Cristo / Le Christ*). That is followed by several hundred pages of improbable conversations arranged by situation. So on p. 267, in a paragraph purported to be taking place in a garden (*Um jardin / Un jardin*) are elements of a conversation that only the most extraordinary circumstances could have made possible:

Allow me to make a bouquet of flowers / Willingly and I will help you / Let's start with roses / Put in some double violets / Don't forget the geranium which smells so good /

Although without a scent, the dahlia is pleasing to the eye / I have some of every colour / Do you like carnations? / Yes, I like to see them, but I don't like the smell / Here's a charming bouquet / All that's missing is some mock orange-blossom.

Or again on p. 199 in a chapter on restaurants (*Uma Casa de pasto* / *Un restaurateur*):

These sweetbreads are too salty / Make us a lettuce salad / And put in some nasturtiums and hard-boiled eggs / This vinegar is worthless / This oil has a very strong smell / But gentlemen, it comes from Italy / Quite possibly, but it must have left its native land a long time ago.

With that last exchange, one senses the pedagogue's temptation to dramatize the conversations, deviating from his primary task. Throughout the text, little pencilled crosses at regular intervals must mark the stages, no doubt daily, by which young Mlle de Campos Vidal learnt what "real" French conversation was like.

The books one buys in second-hand stores, because they have long gone out of print, encourage this kind of discovery. So to take one example, a recent assignment obliged me to re-read a copy of Degas's *Letters* (Grasset edition, 1931) in which I found that one of its previous owners had nit-picking tendencies. On the title page, he or she has written in the date of printing, which in French books is always at the end of the volume; then on p. 61 has crossed out "2500 francs" and replaced it with 3000; has noted on p. 72, after Letter No. XLV, that in fact Letter XCV should have come there; has corrected "Hellen" to "'Helleu" on p. 141; has re-labelled a portrait of Manzi by Degas as "pastel" instead of "oils"; and on p. 229 has judiciously corrected Madame to Mademoiselle, referring to Delphine Tasset, the daughter of the man who supplied the painter's photographical equipment – all of which suggests a certain knowledge of the subject. As for the previous owner of *Mr Degas, bourgeois de Paris* by Georges Rivière, he had a habit of drawing, and could not resist on three occasions reproducing in pencil on the margins or on the back of plates details from a Degas illustration opposite – always with a discreet and fairly sure hand.

The books in my library are like old houses, breathing the presence of the men and women who have lived there in the past, with their sufferings, their loves, their hates, their surprises and disappointments, their hopes and their resignation. On reflection, I have always lived in old buildings myself ...

ACKNOWLEDGEMENTS

Several members of the "bookworm confraternity" have wasted time, which they might have devoted to healthier activities, reading through some of the above or checking details for me. For this and everything else over long years, I thank: Jean-François Barrielle, Pierre Boncenne, Jorge Coli, Pierre-Emmanuel Dauzat, René Hess, Gilles Lapouge, Michel Nadel and Jean-Jacques Terrin.

This book might seem a little unjust about libraries and their staff, who have at different times of my life gone out of their way to be courteous and helpful to me. So I would like to mention as fully as possible those which have provided me with books, and to whom I remain indebted: The Méjanes Library in Aix-en-Provence and the French National Library, as it used to be long ago, in the rue de Richelieu; the Doucet art library in the past, and the ever-welcoming municipal library in La Châtre (Indre) at present.

BIBLIOGRAPHY

[Originals in English or English-language translations of French and other foreign language titles are cited in preference; where no English edition is readily available, the French edition is cited [translated title in brackets]; where possible, the most easily obtainable edition is cited.]

Adams, Laurie Schneider, *The Methodologies of Art* (Westview Press, 1996)

Alpers, Svetlana, *The Art of Describing: Dutch art in the seventeenth century* (John Murray, 1983; Penguin, 1989)

Andrič, Ivo, *Conversation – Goya – Signs*, trans. Celia Hawkesworth and Andrew Harvey (Menard Press/SEES, 1993) [note: the publications in French translation by this author mentioned in the text may cover a somewhat different selection of stories]

Andrič, Ivo, ed. Radmila Gorup, *The Slave Girl and other stories about women* (Central European Press Classics, 2009)

Andrič, Ivo, *Signes au bord du Chemin* [Signs along the road] (L'Age d'homme, 1997)

Andrič, Ivo, *Contes au fil du temps* [Tales down the years] (Le Serpent à Plumes, 2005)

Anon., *The Lascivious Monk* [L'Histoire de Dom B.] (W. H. Allen, 1988)

Ashbee, Henry Spencer, see "Walter"

Auerbach, Erich, *Mimesis*, trans. Willard R. Trask (Princeton University Press, 2003)

Balzac, Honoré de, *Père Goriot*, trans. A. J. Krailsheimer (Oxford University Press, 1999, and other editions)

Balzac, *La Théorie de la démarche* [Theory of walking] (Pandora éditeur, 1978)

Balzac, *Seraphita*, trans. Clara Bell (Dedalus, 1990, and other editions)

Barbey d'Aurevilly, Jules, *The She-Devils*, trans. Jean Kimber (Oxford University Press, 1964 and other editions; sometimes entitled *Les Diaboliques*)

Bassani, Giorgio, *The Garden of the Finzi-Continis*, trans. William Weaver (Harcourt Brace, 1977)

Bassani, Giorgio, *The Heron*, trans. William Weaver (Quartet Encounters/Texas Bookman, 1996)

Baudson, Michel, ed., *L'Art et le temps, regards sur la quatrième dimension* [Art and time: views of the fourth dimension] (Albin Michel, 1985)

Blavier, André, *Les Fous littéraires* [Literary madmen] (Editions des Cendres, 2000)

Bayard, Pierre, *How to Talk about Books You Haven't Read*, trans. Jeffrey Mehlman (Granta, 2008)

Bayard, Pierre, *Sherlock Holmes was wrong: reopening the case of the Hound of the Baskervilles*, trans. Charlotte Mandell (Bloomsbury, 2009)

Bely, Andrey, *Petersburg*, trans. David McDuff (Penguin, 1995)

Bernardin de Saint-Pierre, see Saint-Pierre, J.-F. Bernardin de

Blanchot, Maurice, *The Book to Come*, trans. Charlotte Mandell (Stanford University Press, 2002)

Blunt, Anthony, *Artistic Theory in Italy* (Oxford University Press, 1940, and several later editions)

Blunt, Anthony, *Philibert de l'Orme* (Zwemmer, 1958)

Boman, Patrick, *Dictionnaire de la pluie* [Dictionary of rain] (Seuil, 2008)

Burgess, Anthony and Haskell, Francis, *The Age of the Grand Tour* (Crown, 1967)

Canetti, Elias, *Auto-da-fé*, trans. C. V. Wedgwood (Harvill, 2005)

Chateaubriand, François-René de, *The Memoirs of Chateaubriand*, trans. Robert Baldick (Penguin, 1965)

Clark, Kenneth, *Landscape into Art* (John Murray [1949], 1973, and various editions)

Cocteau, Jean, *Past Tense: Diaries*, vol. 1, trans. Pierre Chanel (Thomson Learning, 1988)

Constant, Benjamin, *Adolphe*, trans. Leonard Tancock (Penguin Classics, 2006)

Constant, Benjamin, *Journal intime précédé du cahier rouge* (Editions du Rocher, 1945)

Cossery, Albert, *The House of Certain Death*, trans. Erik de Mauny (Hutchinson, 1947)

Cossery, Albert, *Men God Forgot*, trans. Harold Edwards (George Leite Circle Edn, 1946)

Cossery, Albert, *The Lazy Ones*, trans. William Goyen (New Directions, 1952)

Cossery, Albert, *If All Men Were Beggars*, trans. P. D. Cummings (McGibbon & Kee, 1957)

Cyrano de Bergerac, Savinien, *Voyages to the Moon and the Sun*, trans. Richard Aldington (Folio Society, 1991, and various other editions)

Dana, Richard, *Two Years Before the Mast. A personal narrative of the sea* ([1840] Penguin Classics, 1981, and various editions.)

D'Arzo, Silvio, *The House of Others*, trans. Keith Botsford (Northwestern University Press, 1995)

Dazai, Osamu, *Setting Sun*, trans. Donald Keene (New Directions, [1958] 1973)

Dazai, Osamu, *No Longer Human*, trans. Donald Keene (New Directions, 1958)

Dehaene, Stanislas, *Reading in the Brain*, no translator listed (Viking, 2009)

De Silva, Anil, *The Art of Chinese Landscape Painting in the Caves of Tun-Huang* (Methuen, 1967)

Diderot, Denis, *Jacques the Fatalist and His Master*, trans. Michael Henry (Penguin, 1986, and other editions)

Didi-Huberman, Georges and Maurizio Gherlardi et al., *Relire Panofsky* [Re-reading Panofsky] (Beaux-Arts de Paris Editions, 2008)

Dominguez, Carlos, *The Paper House*, trans. Nick Caistor (Harvill Secker, 2005)

d'Otremont, Stanislas, *La Polonaise* [The Polish woman] (Julliard, 1957)

Douglas, James, *Catalogus editionum Q. Horatii Flacci, ab ann. 1476 ad ann. 1739* (1739)

Dumas, Alexandre, *The Forty-five Guardsmen*, no trans. mentioned (Dodo Press, 2008, and other editions)

Dumas, Alexandre, *Chico, the Jester*, no trans. mentioned [originally *La Dame de Monsoreau*] (Dodo Press, 2008, and other editions)

Eça de Queiros, José Maria de, *The Maias*, trans. P. M. Pinheiro and A. Stevens ([Bodley Head, 1965] Penguin, 1998)

Elias, Norbert, *What Is Sociology?*, no translator mentioned (Hutchinson, 1978)

Flaubert, Gustave, *Sentimental Education*, trans. Robert Baldick (Penguin, 1970, and other editions)

Foucart-Walter, Elisabeth and Rosenberg, Pierre, *The Painted Cat: the cat in western painting from the fifteenth to the eighteenth century*, no translator mentioned (Rizzoli, 1988)

Friedlander, Max, *From Van Eyck to Bruegel*, trans M. Kay (4th edition, Phaidon, 1981) [note: Brueghel or Bruegel, depending on edition]

Füst, Milan, *The Story of My Wife: the reminiscences of Captain Storr Milan Füst*, trans. Ivan Sanders (Cape, 1989)

Galantaris, Christian, *Manuel de bibliophilie* [Handbook of bibliophilia] (Paris, Editions des Cendres, 1998)

Gay, Sophie, *Ellenore*, 2 vols (The Echo Library, 2008 and various editions)

Gheorgiu, Virgil, *The Twenty-fifth Hour*, trans. Rita Eldon (Knopf, 1950)

Golding, John, *Cubism: a history and an analysis 1907–1914* (Faber, 1959 and various editions)

Gombrich, E. H., *The Story of Art* (Phaidon, 1950, and various editions)

Gonin, Eve, *Le Point de vue d'Ellénore* [Ellénore's point of view] (José Corti, 1981)

Goujon, Jean-Paul and Lefrère, Jacques, *L'Enigme Corneille-Molière* (Fayard, 2006)

Gracq, Julien, *Reading Writing*, trans. not mentioned (Turtle Point Press, 2006)

Guillemin, Henri, *Hugo et la sexualité* [Hugo's sexuality] (Gallimard, 1954)

Hamsun, Knut, *Pan*, trans. James W. Macfarlane (Artemis, 1955 and various editions)

Hamsun, Knut, *August*, trans. Eugene Gay-Tifft ([1932] Howard Fertig, 1990)

Hamsun, Knut, *Benoni*, trans. Arthur Chater (1926)

Hamsun, Knut, *Rosa*, trans. Sverre Lyngstad (Green Integer, 2009)

Hesse, Hermann, *Demian*, trans. W. J. Strachan, (Picador, 1995)

Hesse, Hermann, *Steppenwolf*, trans. Basil Creighton, rev. Walter Sorrell (Penguin, 2001)

Huchon, Mireille, *Louise Labé, une créature de papier* [Louise Labé, a paper creation] (Droz, 2006)

Hugo, Victor, *Carnets, Albums, journaux* (Jean-Jacques Pauvert, 1963)

[Huntington, Gladys], *Madame Solario* ([1956], Penguin, 1978)

Huysmans, J.-K., *Against Nature*, trans. Robert Baldick (Penguin, 1959)

James, Henry, *Hawthorne* (1879)

Japicx, Gysbert, *Tjerne le Frison et autres vers* [Tjerne the Frisian and other verse], trans. and ed. Henk Zwier (Gallimard, l'Aune des peoples Collection, 1994)

Jouve, Pierre-Jean, *Paulina 1880*, trans. R. Letellier and R. Bullen (Northwestern University Press, 1995)

Kafū Nagai, *Rivalry: a Geisha's Tale*, trans. Stephen Snyder (Columbia University Press, 2007) [previous trans. by K. Meissner, 1963]

Kafū Nagai, *La Sumida* [The (river) Sumida] (Gallimard, 1975)

Kaufmann, Emil, *Architecture in the Age of Reason: baroque and post-baroque in England, Italy and France* ([1955] Dover, 1968)

Kazantzakis, Nikos, *Zorba the Greek*, trans. Carl Wildman [1952] (Faber, 2000)

Kennedy, William, *Legs* ([1975] Cape, 1976)

Krleza, Miroslav, *The Banquet in Blitva*, trans. Jasna Levinger-Goy and Edward D. Goy (Northwestern University Press, 2002)

Krleza, Miroslav, *On the Edge of Reason*, trans. Zora Depolo (Quartet, 1987)

Krleza, Miroslav, *The Return of Philip Latinowicz*, trans. Zora Depolo (Quartet, 1989)

Krleza, Miroslav, *Je ne joue plus* [I'm not playing any more] (Seuil, 1970)

Krleza, Miroslav, *Mars, dieu croate* [Mars, a Croatian god] (Calmann-Lévy, 1971)

Krleza, Miroslav, *Les Ballades de Petritsa Kerempuh* [Ballads of Petritsa Kerempuh] (Publications orientalistes de France, 1975)

Krleza, Miroslav, *L'Enterrement à Theresienbourg* [Burial at Theresienburg], trans. into French by Antun Polanscak (Minuit, 1957)

Lafayette, Madame de, *The Princesse de Clèves*, trans. Robin Buss (Penguin Classics, 1992)

Lancastre, Maria José de, no translator mentioned, *Fernando Pessoa: photographic documentation and captions* (Hazan, 1997)

Larbaud, Valery, *200 chambres, 200 salles de bains* [200 bedrooms, 200 bathrooms] (Editions du Sonneur, 2008)

Leblanc, Maurice M. E., *Coffin Island* [an Arsène Lupin adventure], trans. A. Teixera de Mattos (1920)

Levey, Michael, *Painting in Eighteenth-century Venice* ([1959] Yale, 1994, 3rd edition)

London, [John Griffith] Jack, *The Call of the Wild* (1903 and other editions)

Long, Haniel, *The Marvelous Adventure of Cabeza de Vaca* and *Malinche* (Pan interlinear, 1975)

Machado de Assis, Joachim M., *Dom Casmurro*, trans. John Gledson (Oxford University Press, 1997)

Manguel, Alberto, *A History of Reading* (HarperCollins, 1996)

Manguel, Alberto, *A Reading Diary* (Canongate, 2005)

Manguel, Alberto, *The Library at Night* (Yale, 2008)

Marquis, Don, *Anthology: The long lost Tales of Archy and Mehitabel* (UPNE, 1996)

Massing, Jean-Michel, *La Calomnie d'Apelle* [The calumny of Apelles (Mantegna)] (Presses Universitaires de Strasbourg, 1990)

Masters, Edgar Lee, *Spoon River Anthology* (Collier Books, 1956)

Meiss, Millard, *The Painter's Choice: problems in the interpretation of Renaissance art* (Harper & Row, 1976)

Melot, Michel, *La bibliothèque multimédia contemporaine* [The contemporary multimedia library] in the series *Lieux de savoir* (Albin Michel, 2007)

Merceron, Jacques E., *Dictionnaire des saints imaginaires et facétieux* [Dictionary of imaginary and facetious saints] (Le Seuil, 2002)

Miller, Henry, *The Books in My Life* (Peter Owen, 1972)

Miller, Henry, *Time of the Assassins: a study of Rimbaud* (New Directions, 1956; Quartet, 1984)

Monglond, André, *Préromantisme français* [French pre-Romanticism] (Librairie Jose Corti, 1965)

Morand, Paul, *Fancy Goods: Open all Night*, trans. Ezra Pound (New Directions, 1984)

Morand, Paul, *Hecate and Her Dogs*, no translator mentioned (Pushkin Press, 2009)

Morand, Paul, *L'Homme pressé* [The man in a hurry] (Le livre de poche, 1963)

Musil, Robert, *Diaries 1899–1942*, trans. Philip Payne (Basic Books, 1998)

Musil, Robert, *The Man without Qualities*, 2 vols, trans. Sophie Wilkins (Vintage, 1996)

Nabokov, Vladimir, *Pale Fire* ([1962] Everyman, 1992)

Nagai Kafū: see Kafū Nagai

Nodier, Charles, *Mélanges tirés d'une petite bibliothèque* [Gleanings from a small library] (Crapelet, 1829)

Nygren, Anders, *Agape and Eros*, trans. Philip Watson, ([1953], SPCK, 1982)

O'Neill, John P., *Metropolitan Cats* (Metropolitan Museum of Art, 1981)

Painter, George, *Chateaubriand: a biography*. vol. I, *The Longed-for Tempests (1768–93)* (Chatto & Windus, 1977) [NB No second volume published in English either]

Panofsky, Erwin, *Studies in Iconology* ([1939] Harper & Row, 1972)

Polastron, Lucien X., *Books on Fire: The destruction of Libraries throughout history* (Inner Traditions, 2007)

Praz, Mario, *The Romantic Agony*, trans. Angus Davidson (Meridian Books, 1956)

Queneau, Raymond, ed., *Pour une bibliothèque idéale* [The ideal library] (Gallimard, 1956)

Renard, Jules, *L'Ecornifleur* [The scrounger] (Sillage, 2008)

Revel, Jean-François, *The Totalitarian Temptation*, trans. David Hapgood (Secker and Warburg, 1977)

Revel, Jean-François, *Without Marx or Jesus*, trans. J. F. Bernard (MacGibbon and Kee, 1972)

Rivière, Georges, *Mr Degas, bourgeois de Paris* (Librairie Floury, rue de l'Université, 1938)

Rosenblum, Robert. *The Dog in Art: from rococo to post-modernism* (Abrams, 1988)

Saint-Pierre, J. H. Bernardin de, *Paul and Virginia*, trans. Helen Maria
  Williams ([1787] Oxford Woodstock, 1989, and many 19th-century
  editions)

Sanchez, Alberto Ruy, *Mogador: the names of the air*, no translator listed
  (City Lights, 2001)

Sanchez, Alberto Ruy, *The Secret Gardens of Mogador*, trans. Rhonda D.
  Buchanan (White Pine Press, 2009) [note: these appear to be the only
  English translations of the Mogador books]

Shalamov, Varlam, *Kolyma Tales*, trans. John Glad (Penguin, 1994)

Shalamov, Varlam, *Mes Bibliothèques* [My libraries], trans. (from Russian)
  Sophie Benech (Interférences, 1992)

Shōnagon, Sei, *The Pillow Book*, trans. M. McKinney, (Penguin, 2006, and
  various other editions)

Spitzer, Leo, *Linguistics and Literary History: essays in stylistics*, (Princeton
  University Press, 1948)

Starobinski, Jean, *Jean-Jacques Rousseau: Transparency and Obstruction*, trans.
  Arthur Goldhammer (University of Chicago Press, 1988)

Stendhal, [Henri Beyle] *Memoirs of an Egotist*, trans. Andrew Brown
  (Hesperus, 2003 and other versions)

Stendhal, *Life of Henry Brulard*, trans. John Sturrock (Penguin, 1995, and
  other editions)

Stendhal, *Scarlet and Black*, trans. M.R.B Shaw (Penguin, 1993, and other
  editions)

Svevo, Italo, *Confessions of Zeno*, trans. Beryl de Zoete (Penguin, 1976)

Tanpinar, Ahmet Hamdi, *The Time Regulation Institute*, trans. Ender Gurol
  (Turko Tatar Press, 2002)

Teyssèdre, Bernard, *L'Histoire de l'art vue du Grand Siècle* [Art history as seen
  from the *grand siècle* – seventeenth-century France] (René Julliard,
  n.d.)

Torga, Miguel, *Arche*, trans. into French, Claire Cayron (PUF, 1980)

Torga, Miguel, *En franchise intérieure, pages de journal 1933–1977* [Intimate
  frankness, pages from my journal], translated into French by Claire
  Cayron (Aubier Montagne, 1982)

Tristan, Frédéric, *Le Monde à l'envers* [The world upside down] (Hachette,
  1980)

Trollope, Anthony, *An Autobiography* (Oxford University Press, World's Classics, 1980)

Veyne, Paul, *Writing History: essay on epistemology*, trans. Mina Moore-Rinvolucri (Wesleyan, 1984)

Vian, Boris, *Froth on the Daydream*, trans. S. Chapman (Quartet, 1988)

Vicenot, Claude, *Essai de grammaire slovène* [Essay on Slovenian grammar] (Mladinska Knijga, 1975)

"Walter", *My Secret Life*, 11 vols. Originally published anonymously (Amsterdam, 1880s); (and various editions, partial or complete; usually now attributed to Henry Spencer Ashbee, author or editor)

Walter, Henriette and Avenas, Pierre, *L'Etonnante Histoire des noms des mammifères* [The amazing story of the names of mammals] (Robert Laffont, 2003)

Williams, Tennessee, *Four Plays: Summer and Smoke/Orpheus Descending/Suddenly Last Summer/Period of Adjustment* (Signet Classic, 1997, and other editions)

Zorzi, Ludovico, *Représentation picturale et représentation théatrale* [Pictorial and theatrical representation] (Gérard Montfort, 1998)